"Tarnished Gems"

by Marguerite Wellbourne

1.

The house, with the purple front door, was small and slightly shabby, but it was enough for Ruby Grebowski.

It nestled in the middle of a series of terrace houses in Inner Sydney and backed onto a narrow alley, often used as a place for drug addicts to shoot up. At the front, it had a small and untidy front porch. On that porch, a small coffee table shared the space with two wicker chairs that each had a faded and threadbare cushion. The threads of cane on the chairs were worn and broken. Some stuck out like bristles on an unkempt brush.

Ruby had not sat out there since Joseph had died.

Two steps and a short, broken concrete path led to the front gate, which Ruby never used. It opened out onto the road and, like anywhere in Surry Hills, was noisy and, Ruby felt, quite dangerous.

Inside, on the ground floor, it consisted of a small lounge room, which was cluttered with ornaments, books and photographs, a kitchenette, and a bathroom. There was a small entrance hall that was no longer used as such. Ruby had her single bed in there, and she had a curtain rigged up to act as a dividing wall. The main bedrooms were upstairs, but now that she was alone, Ruby had asked her neighbour to bring her bed downstairs so that she didn't have to drag her old bones up the stairs every night. Ruby shuddered to think what the condition of those upstairs rooms was like now. She couldn't bring herself to look. Housework was not a priority any more.

There was a small addition out the back, which used to be the toilet before a modern one was installed inside. Now she used the outside room as a laundry.

Ruby was as happy as a widow of fifteen years could be.

She would often look at the photos of her beloved Joseph, before he got sick. It still hurt, after all these years, that she'd not been able to save him from the cancer that had eaten him away from the inside. Having to watch him become less of a man, Ruby knew, had upset him as much as it had upset her.

There was also a small altar-like setting in the corner of the lounge room, where she tried to keep some fresh flowers. They were often wilted though, now that the garden was non-existent. Finding flowers in this congested area of Sydney wasn't often possible. Small photos graced the shelf, with a few mementoes of her youth, coupled with some pretty crystals. It was a tribute to Joseph, as well as to her brothers and father, who had been executed during the war.

It was that same war that had taken her daughter.

There were so many to grieve for. She still ached inside for all the lives lost, and wondered what had happened to her daughter – she had not seen her since she had been one year old. The altar went a little way towards softening the pain.

These days the only things that kept her company were the TV, her memories and her very spoilt cat, Punch.

She sat on her favourite armchair that was threadbare with age, intermittently watching an old black and white movie with Cary Grant in the leading role, but she had long since lost the thread of the plot.

She quietly dozed on and off, her glasses slipping down her nose as she absently stroked the cat curled up on her lap. Punch was nearly asleep too, but he squirmed and wriggled, got up, turning in circles and kneading her legs with his paws, trying to get more comfortable. Ruby opened her eyes and realised her feet were getting pins and needles in them and she pushed Punch away. He looked at her as if to say 'how dare you' then he sulkily leapt onto the floor, curled himself up on the rug with his back to her and began to snore lightly.

She sat for a moment, fighting the urge to fall asleep again, then heaved herself up and padded over to the kitchenette. Her well-worn slippers made a shushing sound on the faded lino. She put the electric kettle on for a cup of tea, then went over to the tiny fridge, opened it and peered inside. Her glasses slipped a little further down her nose. She muttered to herself as she straightened up and pushed her errant spectacles back into position.

Damn. No milk.

She plodded back through the lounge, parted the curtain, entered her bedroom and looked around. Standing next to the bed, she blinked her eyes with confusion and wondered why she was there.

The kettle whistled loudly and she returned to the kitchen and turned it off. She saw the cup on the bench ready for coffee and remembered she had no milk. By the time she returned to her room, shrugged on her old cardigan and slipped out of her tattered slippers then sat heavily on her bed and put on her walking shoes, fifteen minutes had passed.

She picked up Punch and locked him in the small laundry room. He complained loudly but she ignored him. There was no way she was going to let him have the luxury of her empty rooms while she was out. The last time she had forgotten he was inside, he had shredded her previous pair of slippers.

After she'd grabbed her shopping bag she stood at the back door for a moment and stared at the weeds and broken concrete path in the back yard.

The yard was small and had been neglected since Joseph had died.

He had been so proud of his garden and the abundant crops of vegetables he would harvest from the vegetable patch that he had tended. Now it was a mess. Thistles grew between the cracks in the cement, and dandelion seed heads frothed their seeds into the air whenever there was the slightest breeze. The smell of the cat's leavings permeated the air, although Ruby didn't notice that these days.

Ruby felt her eyes begin to moisten as tears began to form. It was no good – she just had to get on with it. She acknowledged that gardening wasn't her thing, and anyway, it meant nothing now there was no one to share it with – no family, no children, no husband.

She ambled to the gate in the back fence that led to the alley. She looked each way as she shut the gate behind her. There didn't seem to be anyone around, so she stepped out and made her way, passed the graffiti scrawled on all the fences, to the corner.

Cars, some with radios blaring, were bumper to bumper along the main road, and a couple of trucks sat idling at the traffic lights waiting for them to turn green. Fortunately she didn't have to cross the road, so she turned right towards the small shopping area. When she got closer to the shops, the cars were stopped, unable to even creep forwards, and the noise was annoying. A truck began to beep as it reversed into a parking space, holding up the traffic even more. Someone shouted at the driver and many drivers honked their horns. The truckie made a rude sign and continued parking, in spite of them all. He just did his job, knowing he had to deliver his load to a particularly irascible shop-owner.

She simply turned her hearing aid down a little and trudged on, one step at a time. It wasn't far to the local shops but Ruby needed to concentrate, as the pavement was crooked and broken in places. Trees planted along the roadside had grown tall, pushing the concrete up with their roots.

She wandered past the local park and stopped to look so she could catch her breath.

It was one of the wonders of this busy city that never ceased to amaze Ruby. The parks were dotted throughout the suburbs, even here, so close to the city centre. She watched several children playing a game of chase, shrieking as they ran. Under the shade of the huge trees along the eastern border a few students clustered in a semicircle, their books open and their faces a study in concentration. A handful of adult executives were taking the opportunity to have a break and one lay with his hands behind his head, obviously taking a snooze, away from the pressures of the office. A couple meandered down a nearby path, stopping and kissing, quite oblivious to anyone else around them.

Ruby noticed two horses being ridden around the circuit. One was a chestnut and the other, slightly smaller, had appaloosa type colouring. She smiled to herself. Aaah! When she was young, before the war, she had had a pony. The country village just outside Stuttgart in Germany had been pretty and her family had enjoyed the idyllic atmosphere. A farmer, down the road from their block of flats, had let her keep a pony on agistment. She often rode it after school.

She frowned. It was a shame. She couldn't even remember its name now.

She stood for a while, lost in her memories, then moved slowly on.

By the time she arrived at '*Farid's Deli*' she was puffed again, and needed to sit down.

Farid came out from behind the counter and took the old lady's arm and led her to a seat near the rear of the shop.

"You know if you want anyt'ing you should send me a phone call," he said in a heavy accent. "I would put my boy on his bike to deliver, you know."

Ruby smiled. She didn't have the heart to tell him she had cancelled her phone, that she could no longer afford it now that she was on the pension.

"I know," she said, "but it doesn't hurt me to get out occasionally." She stopped and took a deep breath. "God knows I haven't got anything else to do!"

Farid nodded. "Yes," he agreed. "It is difficult world when you are alone. Even when you're not, it'sa not easy!" He waved his hand towards the shelves of small-goods. "I sometimes wonder whether all this is worth it, you know! This part of town often is dangerous. Had brick thrown through the window last year, now I have the bars to save my stock." He shook his head dejectedly. "I worry about the wife and children out there in this strange world since the Twin Tower t'ing happened."

Ruby nodded. "Everyone is scared of everybody, these days. It doesn't seem possible it was four years ago already." She shook her head unhappily. "The terrorists have definitely won, in my opinion."

For a few minutes they discussed the woes of the world, although Ruby did most of the listening and added little to the conversation. Then another customer came in and took Farid away from Ruby. She sat staring into space, contemplating her life and the inevitable conclusion of that life that was awaiting her before too long.

After a while, she sighed, got up, waited for Farid to serve her, picked up her milk and wearily began the trip home.

When she got to the park, she stopped and rested, looking for the riders on the two horses. She saw them coming around the back of the park. The two girls were animated and laughing. One of them waved to a couple of lads who hadn't been there when Ruby had passed earlier. The girls were giggling and calling to them, obviously showing off to catch the boys' attention.

As they drew nearer, a car on the road behind Ruby, backfired.

BANG!

The noise made Ruby jump as if a gun had gone off. After all this time, she still reacted badly to sudden noises. She blinked rapidly, trying to calm her racing heart. Amazing how something so inconsequential could remind her of the war, of the horrors that had happened to her, her family and her friends.

The loud and sudden noise also affected the young riders and their horses. Both horses shied. Each rider needed to concentrate and were having some trouble getting the horses under control. One of them was particularly spooked. It was obviously upset and so was its rider.

Ruby stood still and continued to watch. A young man sauntered towards them. Ruby heard one of the girls laugh and call out something. The horses were still unsettled. The man waved. The girl with the blonde curls ignored her friend, who was still trying to get her horse under control. She continued to laugh and flirt with the man, keeping her back to her friend.

The car back-fired again.

BANG! BANG!

Suddenly the brunette's horse reared up, and its rider lost her grip and fell off. Ruby watched as the girl hit her head on the concrete pathway and lay ominously still. The young man ran towards the rearing horse, trying to grab the reins. If the hooves landed on the girl, there would be serious consequences. The other girl turned her horse and froze in position. When the young man had grabbed the reins and quietened the frightened horse he led the appaloosa over to the chestnut, taking the reins from the blonde's shaking hands as she sat still immobilised with shock. As he led the horses over to a grassy area he turned and spoke.

"See to your friend," he said, "I'll look after the horses."

"Thanks, Brad." The girl came out of her trance and slid off the horse, then flew towards her friend who was lying on the ground. She knelt beside her and burst into tears.

For Ruby, the sounds of the traffic, the call of a lone bird and the murmur of conversations from the others in the park, all faded into a stifling silence.

Everything seemed shrouded in a fog. Ruby was only focused on the prone figure of the girl on the ground. She heard the other rider cry out and as she watched, the girl jumped off her mount, ran to her friend and bent over the inert body.

Later, how she got to the girl, Ruby wasn't sure. She moved her old and sore limbs as if she was once again an agile youth. The milk carton flew unnoticed from her hand and fell with a thud onto the path, spraying milk everywhere.

By the time she reached the figure on the ground, the other girl was crying, hands covering her face. She hadn't done anything, and seemed unable to think rationally. She kept rocking backwards and forwards, speaking incoherently, whether to herself or her friend, Ruby didn't know.

Ruby went to her and shook her gently.

"Call the ambulance," she said gently to the kneeling figure.

The girl lifted her tear-stained face.

"OK." She mumbled. She got up and moved a little distance away, still sobbing. She felt in her pockets for her mobile. Tears were blurring her vision, and the lump in her throat was threatening to choke her. She turned towards her friend who lay on the ground, watching the old lady who was now bent over her. She gulped back her sobs and called the emergency number.

Ruby knelt by the prone body of the girl's friend and tried to get a response. She knew there was a problem because the young girl had murmured, her eyes flickering, then curled into a foetal position. When the girl's eyes opened and looked at Ruby there was a strange blankness. The fact that she had her thumb in her mouth and was sucking it wasn't normal either.

"It's OK." Ruby crooned. "The ambulance is on it's way." At least she hoped it was. When she looked around, she saw that the other girl had her mobile phone glued to her ear and seemed to be doing more sobbing and hiccuping into it than anything else.

By this time, the young man had taken both the horses to the grass and they were now contentedly munching the rich green lawn as if nothing had happened. He walked over and put his hand on the friend's shoulder as she finished speaking on the mobile. He spoke and she nodded distractedly, and began to move back to Ruby. Then she stopped, put her hand over her mouth and began to sob again. A small crowd had gathered and everyone was silently watching. Nobody offered any help. A couple of the younger children began to wail, and their mothers hurriedly whispered to them to be quiet.

Ruby wasn't interested in any of them. She neither glanced up nor even appeared to hear. She was more worried about the girl.

The girl on the ground took her thumb out of her mouth and glared at Ruby.

"Go away!" she snarled. "I'm fine! Who are you?"

Her friend sidled up.

"Her name's Jade," the girl said timidly to Ruby, "And I'm Sapphire, but all my friends call me Saffy. Is she OK?"

Once again the girl on the ground glared, at her friend this time, now edged with puzzlement. Her voice was getting weaker.

"Who are you? Where am I? Leave me alone!" She tried to get up but couldn't summon the energy or get her legs to obey her desire.

Ruby suddenly heard the wail of a siren. Her relief was palpable. She let out her breath in a rush, unaware that she had been holding it. She hoped the sound was the ambulance for them and that it was coming to help, and quickly.

"Go to the gates of the park," she directed the still sobbing friend. "Guide the ambulance to us – they'll need to get here as quickly as possible. Your friend is coming round again and is beginning to struggle to get up – I need the medics here now."

Jade's eyes flickered open.

She spoke, in a little voice. "I feel sick!"

Ruby tried to move her carefully onto her side. Jade wasn't helping. Her body was limp and her eyes continued to look glazed.

***

Saffy still hovered nearby. She seemed in a state of shock, and Ruby wanted to help her, too. At this point Jade began to convulse.

"Are you sure – she isn't going to die, is she?" Saffy hesitated and took a deep breath, her eyes red from weeping. She looked as if she was ready to burst into tears again.

"She's fine!" Ruby was holding Jade's head, and slowly the spasms passed. "I'm Ruby," she said over her shoulder to Saffy, "and I live on Cleveland Street with the purple door " She fumbled around in her pocket and pulled out a scrap of paper – an old shopping list. She called out to the crowd.

"Anyone got a pencil?"

A hand offered her one and she scribbled on the piece of paper, handing it to Saffy and giving back the pencil. Saffy stuffed it into her bra.

Ruby looked back at Jade. "I'll talk to you after Jade here is in the ambulance. But go! Look for the ambulance and guide it over here when it arrives. It should be here any minute."

Jade sank back into unconsciousness, and lay still, her face going pale. Saffy looked at her as if she was seeing a ghost.

"Go! Quick!" Ruby repeated.

Saffy turned, reluctantly, but then, as if she had finally got control and understanding, began to run to the entrance gates.

Ruby once more focused on the girl on the ground. Her eyes had closed and the thumb was back in her mouth. Ruby was beginning to feel slightly hysterical beneath her calm exterior, and she wished the ambulance would hurry up and arrive. She realised the severity of the situation. She fleetingly saw, in her mind's eye, her friends from her village in Germany being crowded together by soldiers and her reaction to the trauma in front of her and her recollections began to cause her body to tremble. She bit down on her lip and shook the memories away. Jade needed her now. If she weren't careful she would need the ambulance, too.

It seemed forever before the ambulance arrived next to Ruby and Jade.

They say that when shock begins, time slows down and that is exactly what seemed to happen. For Ruby, the paramedics appeared to amble across from the vehicle. One of them stood quietly and asked Ruby what had happened. The other was checking Jade. Ruby tried to control her impatience, knowing that they were trained personnel and were able to stay calm in an emergency. It wasn't working for Ruby – she felt consumed with worry.

Somehow she told them what she had witnessed, how she had acted and what she had done, which, in Ruby's mind, was precious little. Then she told them what Jade had seemed like, what she had said and how puzzled and yet aggressive she had been. It seemed strange, because Ruby didn't think the ambulance driver and his partner had rushed or been doing anything except speaking to her. However, by the time Ruby had finished talking, Jade was already in the ambulance. The medic looked at the old lady and patted her hand, looking at her with concern.

"Thank you," he said. "You did very well. You look as if you could do with some help yourself. Are you all right?"

Ruby nodded. She had no intention of being a burden. It had been ingrained in her during the war – admit to nothing, keep silent and you would be safe. So, even though her voice was a little scratchy and she needed to sit down, she told them she was fine and that Saffy, Jade's friend should go with them in the ambulance. They looked for her, but Saffy was nowhere in sight.

***

Once the ambulance had arrived and the paramedics were looking after Jade, Saffy watched them as one of the medics talked to the old lady. Jade was put on a stretcher, and wheeled carefully into the ambulance. From her position behind the small gathering of people who were drawn to the scene of the accident, she craned her neck to see what was happening. Saffy couldn't see any movements as the stretcher was placed in the vehicle. Her friend's body seemed so still. Something wasn't right. Jade had been talking, but now she was deathly pale. Saffy felt a welling up of panic, and inched back into the bushes growing along the edge of the park. She hid there until the ambulance left then she scuttled away.

***

Ruby looked around for Saffy.

"Her friend was with her, and that young man over there looking after the horses was a witness, too."

At least that's what she thought she said. She didn't remember the paramedics talking to anyone else but her, but they must have. They must have searched for Saffy and asked people in the crowd what had happened.

Ruby wanted to tell Saffy where she lived. She wanted to find out about Jade's family. She wanted to see Saffy again. She wanted to comfort her and let her know that Jade was in the best possible hands.

Saffy seemed to have disappeared.

Saffy had asked Ruby where she lived, and Ruby thought she had told her, but she wasn't sure. It was all a bit of a muddle.

Ruby watched as the ambulance move away, then she relaxed and shock really set in. A caring young lady from the crowd helped Ruby to a nearby park bench. Someone else asked her if she would like a drink, and a bottle of water miraculously appeared in front of her. Another person pushed a carton of milk into her hands.

"I saw you drop your milk," a voice said out of the crowd. "The carton split and milk went everywhere. I got you a new one."

Ruby looked up and thanked whoever it was. She didn't know. She couldn't see. Her eyes wouldn't focus and she became aware that she was crying – not gulping, heart wrenching sobs – just a river of tears leaking out of her eyes and running down her wrinkled and soft cheeks.

Slowly the crowd dispersed. One University student came and sat next to Ruby on the bench and held her hand, making soothing sounds until Ruby had begun to settle.

"Do you live far away?" asked the concerned young man. "I'll walk you home, if you like. Do you need me to call a doctor?"

Ruby shook her head.

"I'll be right in a moment," she said with another sigh. "My old bones don't like all this worry," she added. "But they've seen worse."

After several more minutes, the student stood up.

"I'm sorry," he said. "But I have to go. My lessons start again in a few moments. Are you sure you'll be OK? I can walk you home if you want me to."

"That's OK." Ruby smiled carefully. She could feel tears ready to fall again, and she took a deep breath to control the feeling. "Off you go. I'll sit here for a while. I'll be fine."

The young man walked away reluctantly, turning every now and again to look and check on Ruby. She smiled and waved him away.

Finally everyone was gone. Ruby looked around. Nobody was watching.

She stood, wincing slightly, and turned towards home. Her back was sore and her feet felt as if she had run a marathon. Her home seemed liked a million miles away. She gritted her teeth.

"One step at a time", she thought, *"I'll be fine. Just keep moving!"*

It took her quite a long time to walk home. She needed to stop several times along the way to rest and breathe. Even the sight of the graffiti on her neighbour's fence was welcome, because by then her head was thumping and her legs were aching. It meant she was nearly home. She staggered a few more steps.

At last she opened her back gate and reached the sanctuary of her home. She got to the laundry, let Punch out, wrinkling her nose at the smell. She'd have to clean up the mess later. Punch always pooped in the laundry when she shut him in there, as if he was punishing her for his imprisonment. She let Punch into the kitchen. Better by far to have him cranky than letting him roam and perhaps losing him altogether. She closed the laundry door and ignored the problem.

When she got inside, she put the milk in the fridge and made her way to the lounge.

The coffee was forgotten.

She collapsed into her comfortable chair.

Everything ached.

Everything hurt.

Even her emotions were all awry.

She was exhausted.

For the first time in a very long time, she became aware just how terribly and painfully alone she was. Even Punch, rubbing up against her legs, didn't help the expanding hurt in her chest.

2.

Saffy couldn't believe what had happened. She watched the ambulance drive away as she stood in the shadow of the trees.

It took her friend with it.

Even though Ruby had suggested that she should go in the ambulance, she just hadn't been able to face it.

She saw Ruby being led to a bench by some of the students. She saw the man, Brad, walk away holding the reins of the two horses.

It was surreal.

Saffy felt as if she was overlooked in the tragedy that had unfolded, an accessory that wasn't part of the drama. The fact that she had hidden away as everyone looked for her didn't make her feel any different. She felt that no one cared about her. Her stomach was tied up in knots and she was scared for Jade. Even so her child within was crying out – *What about me?*

And that was a contradiction anyway. She really had wanted to hide, conceal herself away from the curious crowds that seemed to thrive on bad luck. She didn't want to answer the questions about the incident. She wasn't ready, in her present state of shock, to confront Jade's family, who she presumed would blame her for the accident. After all, she had ignored Jade while she flirted with Brad, even though she knew Jade was having difficulties. She'd even laughed – telling Brad that Jade wasn't much of a rider. Now her guilt and shock pushed her over the edge into paranoia.

She crept away. Thank goodness she had asked for Ruby's address. At the moment she couldn't remember what Ruby had told her. Later, when she felt better, she would go and thank the old lady for her help.

A thought slithered into her mind. What if Ruby had just been an interfering old busy body? If she saw Saffy as the villain, looked at her with accusations in her eyes. What if she knew Saffy had caused the accident?

Yes. That was it. Ruby knew. She'd seen the whole thing. She must know that it was Saffy's fault that this terrible thing had happened.

Saffy stopped then. She sat down right where she was, in the middle of the path. And sobbed, and sobbed, and sobbed.

It was her fault.

If she hadn't been bored. If she hadn't called Jade to come with her to the park. If she hadn't owned two horses that she stabled there. If she hadn't told her to wave at Brad, the guy Jade liked. If she hadn't tried to show off to the group of young lads that had come into the park only moments before. If she hadn't ignored the skittishness of her friend's horse. If she had helped instead of talking to Brad. If she… If she …

Her brain kept going around and around – circles of guilt, circles of regret, circles of worry.

No one stopped and spoke to her. Legs hurried past, skirting around Saffy as if she was some flotsam dredged up from the gutter. There were so many drug addicts and drunks in the area that the people had become cautious of strangers around here. Fear of involvement infused each person who hurried along the path.

It took some time, but eventually Saffy controlled herself. She looked up and noticed that she had wandered into the shopping area, some way from the park.

Her mind was in a turmoil of self-loathing, yet she felt the need for some type of comfort. It was no use getting it from her mother. Her mother, Topaz, had never been much of a help. She seemed unable to give the succour Saffy needed. Saffy thought she probably hadn't wanted her anyway. She was sure she'd been an accident, the result of a one-night stand sometime in the past. As far as Saffy knew, her father was only a sperm donor, lost in the crowd of men Topaz had known.

Saffy thought about her mother. Topaz had never appeared to love her. She was a singer of some renown, working most evenings, rehearsing most days. She never seemed to be around – certainly never sat with her and actually talked.

Saffy didn't care.

What was the point? Now she was a wanted criminal.

Hang on. Where had that thought come from? Saffy looked around at the people rushing to and fro, caught up in their own worlds, not seeing her standing there. It was like she was in a bubble, invisible to everyone.

She walked over to a café and rummaged around in her pockets. She found a fifty-dollar note. At least her mother kept her supplied with money.

A waiter came over to her. Saffy ordered a cappuccino and a slice of cheesecake. As she waited, she appeared to stare at the furniture in the window of the store opposite.

She didn't see anything there.

What she did see was Jade, lying still and crumpled on the ground. She saw the old woman, Ruby, who had looked after Jade. She saw herself, while sitting frozen with indecision, rocking backwards and forwards, like a demented statue. She felt the hurt, when Ruby had sent her away to call the ambulance, as if she was nothing but a nuisance.

She hadn't known what to do at the time. It had all been so overwhelming.

She went over and over the incident in her mind. The more she sat and thought, the worse it got. Now she realised what the problem was.

Jade was dead.

That was the only explanation.

Her brain screamed the accusation.

"Oh my God! I've killed my best friend."

Saffy shook the thought away. It was ridiculous.

But it niggled there, like a demon.

Saffy got up and walked away from the café table. She saw nothing, no one. Her eyes were glazed and her body was working on autopilot.

The waiter walked towards her with her coffee and cake, but she didn't see him. He watched her, shaking his head with disgust. *"That's what you get when you take an order from a druggie,"* he thought *"Well, at least I got her money."*

He turned back to the counter, placing the cup and plate behind the cash register. Should he run after her and give her the money back? Well, at least, give her her change? He went back to the table where she had been sitting and looked up and down the street. She was already out of sight.

She wasn't at the café. She wasn't walking along the street. She wasn't in Surry Hills. She wasn't even in Sydney. She certainly wasn't amongst friends. She had no friends.

She was in torment.

She continued to walk. Where she was going she didn't know. All she could think about was the death of her friend.

Slowly a plan began to gel inside her head. Now she knew what she must do. She would find the witnesses. She would make sure they would never talk.

She stood up straight. At least she knew where to start. The first thing she had to do was find the old lady. Ruby, wasn't it?

Saffy couldn't think of any other option. The old lady was old, but she needed to talk to her. Let her know it wasn't her fault, it wasn't…it wasn't!

She didn't want her to tell the authorities anything that might put the blame onto her.

She had to kill her. Stupid thought!

That was horrible. The worst thought she had ever had. And the most idiotic. But what if something was said and then she would be in jail before she knew it. She hadn't even had a life. She wanted a life.

No – she definitely had to talk to her – convince her that it was just an accident.

She patted herself down. Where had she put the address? Was it in her pockets?

The slip of paper tucked into her bra tickled and scratched. This was it. She pulled the creased and dirty piece of paper out of its hiding place and unfolded it.

All it had on it was 'Ruby Grebowski, Cleveland Street, Surry Hills'.

Admittedly Ruby had scribbled it in a hurry, and told her she would talk after Jade was in the ambulance, but why had she forgotten to write the number down?

Shit! It wasn't much help. Cleveland Street was a long road!

She had hoped that she could go in, do what she had to do to protect herself, not be noticed, then disappear into the urban anonymity around 'The Rocks' or 'The Cross' area.

It was a dilemma.

If she asked too many questions, people would know! But she didn't have much time, and she couldn't think of any other solution. Mind you, perhaps she was over-reacting. How silly to be thinking of killing people! She had already rejected that thought. She would get into even more trouble.

No! She would just have to find her and explain that it wasn't really her fault. Make Ruby understand that she was too young to go to jail. Gosh she was only seventeen. Her conscience answered her – "*Yes, and Jade was only seventeen, too. Too young to die!*"

Cleveland Street was long and full of terrace houses, some of them like rabbit warrens, housing five, six or more people at a time.

She glanced around. Was she near Cleveland Street?

A woman came striding out of the door next to Saffy and nearly bumped into her.

"Oh! What are you doing here?"

Saffy was astonished. She had walked all the way to the real estate office where Jade's mother worked. She stood still, her face a study of surprise.

Jewel spoke again. "I asked you – what are you doing here?" Saffy could hear the exasperation in the woman's voice. She had never particularly liked Jade's mother, and thought the feeling was reciprocated.

Did she know what had happened? Was she going to grab her and take her to the police? She should run, but her legs wouldn't obey the command. Finally she found the courage to speak.

"Um," she cleared her throat and tried to look innocent. "Are you off to the hospital?"

"I beg your pardon?" Jewel looked at Saffy as if the girl had gone slightly mad.

Saffy grimaced. She obviously hadn't heard and now she had to tell her. She wouldn't admit to anything though. And she wouldn't tell her that she thought that Jade was dead either. She didn't want to be dragged off to the police station right now. Besides, she knew Jewel well enough that she would make a scene and everyone in the street would know. She would become the centre of attention and she would shrivel inside from humiliation.

She smiled, although there was no warmth in her eyes.

"Haven't you heard?" she said. "I was coming to tell you." Hopefully Jewel wouldn't notice the about face of her statement.

Jewel lifted a well-defined eyebrow. "And?"

"Jade's been taken to hospital. She…she had an accident. She fell off the horse. Banjo reared and…" Saffy spilt the words in the rush to get it over with, waiting for the explosion from Jewel.

Jewel went absolutely still.

"Is it serious?" she asked.

Saffy didn't know what to say. She didn't want to make matters worse, but Jewel looked as if she was annoyed by the interruption and wanted to be on her way. In all conscience, Saffy knew she had to at least say that Jewel should go and find out. She was far too frightened to tell her anymore.

She tried to couch her words, so that Jade's mother wasn't too shocked.

"Apparently she was unconscious when they put her in the ambulance."

Jewel looked furious.

"For goodness sake, girl. Was she or wasn't she? Were you there?"

Saffy stared at Jewel, but didn't say a word. She didn't know what to say. She certainly didn't want to tell Jewel that in all probability her daughter was dead.

Jewel sighed crossly. "Well, I suppose I'd better go and see her then. Though I'd really prefer to go and see the buyers I've got a meeting with, first." She turned, stuck her head around the door of the office and spoke to her boss. "David, can you ring the Forsyths and tell them my daughter has been taken to hospital and I'll have to make other arrangements to take them through the house at Point Piper?"

"My goodness, is she all right?" David stood and walked up to Jewel, looking most concerned.

"I'm sure it's nothing!" Jewel rolled her eyes. "You know how teenage girls like to be such drama queens!" David was lost for words, and before he could ask anything more, Jewel turned back to Saffy.

"Which hospital?" she asked.

Saffy stuttered out the answer, hoping she had got it correct. Her brain was in such a whirl and she felt confused and a little panicky.

"Come on," Jewel ordered, "Into the car – you might as well come with me."

Saffy hurriedly shook her hands in front of her, as if she was warding off a swarm of mosquitoes.

"Um! No, no. It's OK. I've got to go! I have to get something for Mum." And with that she hurried away leaving Jewel tut-tutting and complaining under her breath. Jewel was clearly annoyed and she strode towards her work car that was parked just around the corner from the real estate agent's premises.

However, by the time she got in, fastened her seat belt and started the car, she had already dismissed Saffy from her mind. She was more interested in working out how to mend the broken appointment with the Forsyth's. Her brow furrowed as she thought of her daughter. Jade was the most important thing in her life – which is why she worked so hard. *"Please let her be alright."*

She turned into the traffic and silently cursed Jade's timing. This sale would have given her the biggest commission than she had ever had. They would have been almost set for life.

She swore under her breath, as a driver loudly sounded the horn and there was a screech of brakes. It was more important to concentrate on her driving as she wove her way through the traffic. Some of the driver's around here were just plain crazy!

***

Saffy had taken the opportunity to disappear when Jewel spoke to David, but she had only gone a short way away. She watched through the window of the dress shop she had scuttled into. The dresses were cotton, multi-coloured caftan-style dresses from India, and she had no intention of buying one. However, when she saw Jewel drive away, she took a couple of the dresses and disappeared into the fitting rooms at the back of the shop.

She drew the curtain across and sat down on the floor with her back to the mirror. She stared at the curtain. It had a strange tweedy texture and she wondered why that suddenly seemed so interesting. She sat there for a long time.

She vaguely heard voices.

"She's been in there a long time," one of the voices said.

"I think you ought to check on her, Shirl," the other woman said. "I don't like someone being in there more than ten minutes, and she's been in there about twenty minutes now!"

Saffy became aware that footsteps were coming towards her. The shop assistant knocked discreetly on the wood outside the cubicle.

"Are you all right in there?" she asked.

Saffy didn't answer. Her face was still contorted with worry, her cheeks showing the streaks of more tears she hadn't realised she'd shed. She stood up in a hurry, left the dresses on the floor, brushed passed the assistant and rushed out of the shop.

Everyone seemed to be against her.

She was very scared and felt so alone.

Once she was outside on the street she tried to think what she should do next. There was no way she was going to the hospital to be told bluntly that Jade was dead and that she would be taken into custody for the murder. There was also no going home, either. Lately, her mother didn't seem to care. She was more interested in her current flame and Saffy couldn't even remember his name.

She looked up and down the street, ignoring the stares of the hurrying people around her. She had no idea where to go.

She began to walk.

Nowhere in particular – she just walked. It was more crucial that she took herself further and further away from the scene of the accident. Further and further away from her guilt. Further and further away from the accusations in her brain.

She walked for hours.

Suddenly she realised it was getting dark, and she looked around with awareness for the first time all day.

She was under the bridge. Sydney Harbour Bridge, the 'coat-hanger' as it was called. It loomed above her. The sound of peak hour traffic and trains above her head echoed loudly in the space. The huge columns supporting this part of the bridge made her feel insignificant.

She found a spot near the harbour, sheltered by these massive columns, curled up in as small a ball as possible and fell asleep from exhaustion and delayed shock.

***

When the sun hit her face the next morning, she couldn't believe she had slept all night, and so soundly that nothing had woken her.

She stood and stretched. Her muscles were sore. She looked about, still feeling a bit dazed. It was cold and a little windy. No one was around.

Without warning, the memories of yesterday's events flooded back into her mind. She scrunched up her face and closed her eyes tightly, but the pictures of Jade on the ground were still there. All she wanted to do was run away. Stop the images in her mind.

She began to walk once more. Walking to ease the pain and guilt inside her.

Then her stomach rumbled. She realised she was hungry, very hungry. She once more checked the pockets of her jeans. Ruby's piece of paper with the address on it was stilled tucked into her bra, but the money was gone.

"Shit! That's right! I left the café without my change! Bugger I didn't even drink the coffee!"

Her brain went a million miles an hour, but she wasn't getting anywhere. Again, she screwed up her eyes, gritted her teeth and shook her head. Well, there was nothing for it – she would just have to get some food and drink.

She knew that she should make her way back to some where near the café that had been in Oxford Street, so she began the long journey back the way she had come last night.

Now that she was awake, she was able to look around and understand where she was.

It was still very early, but the city was beginning to come alive. She saw other young people on the streets, carrying backpacks and running their fingers through their hair as if they had just woken up, like her.

Several shops were already open. The newsagency near the corner was doing a brisk trade as workers began to filter off the train stations and buses. Coffee shops and breakfast bars opened their shutters like slow eyelids, ready for another busy day. A garbage truck came slowly down the road, collecting the bins, clunking them up to the top and emptying them noisily into the gaping hole that would eat the contents.

She needed food, too.

She thought about going to her grandmother's. Pearl lived in Parramatta, but Saffy decided against it. She didn't have money for a train or bus ticket. Besides, there was every possibility that the police had already alerted Pearl that Saffy was wanted.

Her stomach burbled again, this time more loudly. She looked around, wondering if anyone else had heard the noise. She put her hand over her stomach as if to mask the grumble.

She needed food now.

Not far away, a middle aged Asian woman stood at a bus stop. The woman was holding a green recycled bag from a supermarket chain. She had obviously been shopping early, and Saffy could see a bag of apples on the top, almost bursting out.

She strode up to the lady and stood behind her. With a slight shove from her knees, she knocked the bag.

"Sorry," she murmured to the lady, patting her on the shoulder. The bag of apples overbalanced and several fell onto the pavement. Saffy quickly squatted down. She felt bad taking from this woman, but she needed something to eat, and she couldn't think of anything else, and she was hungry *now*.

"Sorry," she said again. "Here, let me help you."

She scooped the apples together and placed them in the bag, keeping one in the folds of her jacket.

The woman turned. "T'ank you," she said. Then to make Saffy feel even worse, the woman handed her one of the apples.

No words were spoken, but, keeping her eyes downcast, Saffy took the apple and nodded. As she began to walk away, the bus arrived and when she looked back, the bus drove off and the woman was gone.

***

All morning, Saffy wandered around, looking into shops, keeping to the shadows. She munched on the apples while she sat on a bench near an entrance to the train station. She walked along the part of a path near Darling Harbour. She wandered down Elizabeth Street, losing herself in the crowds of shoppers. She sat on the grass in the park overlooking Central Station and watched the trains coming and going on the plethora of tracks below her. Finally she snoozed in the shade.

When she finally awoke, she noticed she was near Cleveland Street. She walked along the road, looking at all the terrace houses, wondering which one was the old lady's. She had a feeling there was more information Ruby had given her, but she couldn't remember what it was. She crossed over the railway bridge and realised she was in Redfern. She didn't think this would be where Ruby lived, so she turned and walked back.

It didn't seem possible that the day was almost over. Saffy found it hard to believe that she had made it through the whole day without being caught. As the day died and the sun sank below the buildings, the cool night air rolled in across the waters of the harbour. Saffy crossed at the traffic lights and made her way along a side street. In the darkness she realised she was hungry again so she turned and made her way to Oxford Street.

When she arrived there she was on the opposite side of the road to a café. This part of Sydney was bristling with eateries. Every second shop was a snack bar, coffee lounge or restaurant. They were all busy. Even though it was now well after seven o'clock, there were still a lot of people coming and going.

She crossed the road. A couple of cars sped by, and she skipped hurriedly out of the way when the driver of one of them held his hand on the horn and seemed to leave it there for five minutes. She put her finger up and poked out her tongue! He yelled some obscenity to her but she was out of hearing range and didn't hear, or at least, pretended she didn't hear.

She sat at one of the outside tables working out some sort of a scheme.

If she ordered some food, she could make a run for it before they gave her a bill. She went inside the shop and casually picked a soft drink from the fridge, then went back outside and waited. While she drank from the can, she checked out the next door shops and any alleyways that were close by. She made a mental note to go left along the street when she made her dash. When the waiter asked, she ordered a meal.

It took all of her patience to sit still without fidgeting, until the food arrived. When it did, she ate it as if she hadn't eaten for a week. The waiter came and slipped the bill onto the table next to her. She kept her eyes down, and as soon as he went back inside, she shoved the last forkful of food in her mouth, then stood and ran.

She heard someone come out of the shop and begin to run after her, calling out. She didn't turn. She just ran. It seemed to be all she was doing lately.

3.

By the time Jewel got to the hospital, she was seething. She had spent a lot of time nurturing her relationship with Mr and Mrs Forsyth. Anyone wanting to buy at Point Piper was at the high end of the market, and the commission she would get was huge. Now Jade had put a spoke in her carefully constructed wheel, and, knowing her boss David like she did, she figured he'd probably take over and get the commission instead. She grimaced. Even though she slept with him, she knew that when it came to business and what would go into their individual bank accounts, it was gloves off!

Anyway, she didn't know what was going on. Inside, her heart was thundering. She was worried. Saffy hadn't given her much information, other than the name of the hospital, and then she'd fled using some excuse about her mother.

The hospital was crowded. Jewel looked around. It seemed to her that all the flotsam and jetsam of life were in the foyer. There were people wandering around with their pyjamas on, wheeling the steel poles of drips, with tubes disappearing into embarrassing places. Several families congregated around a gentleman in a wheelchair, with children running around and their parents seemingly taking no notice of them. It was enough to make even the strongest person feel queasy!

She strode up to the reception desk and looked around. The area was not manned. The deep-seated worry about her daughter had been converted into anger and she stood, drumming her fingers on the desktop and tapping her foot loudly.

A young woman came panting up to the desk.

"Sorry, Madam," she gasped. "There was an emergency in the foyer – a lady fainted, fell and hit her head."

"That's no excuse." Jewel snapped. "I don't need to hear all the details. You shouldn't have left your desk. I'm looking for Jade Sutcliffe. I'm her mother. Which ward and room is she in?"

The girl behind the counter smiled, covering up her irritation. She had been working here for several years, and knew that tragedy and worry brought out the worst in some people. She had learnt to keep calm and just give them the information and let them go. There were so many other nice moments that the sooner she moved this particular lady on, the better she could focus on other things. She checked the computer.

She looked into Jewel's piercing blue eyes, and said, quite calmly.

"Room 15, Ward 7 on the second floor, Madam."

Jewel didn't say a word, not even a word of thanks or a nod of acceptance; she just walked away towards the lifts. The receptionist felt like making a face and saying something rather sarcastic, but another woman, who was holding the hand of a cute curly-haired little girl, walked up to the desk. The woman timidly asked a question while the little girl wriggled and tried to escape her mother's grasp. The receptionist was still smarting over Jewel's attitude and didn't hear what she had been asked.

"Pardon?' she said. Before the woman repeated the question, they both turned to watch Jewel get on the lift, each woman giving a sigh of relief as she disappeared.

Back to her job.

The woman with the child raised an eyebrow.

"I don't know how you put up with being spoken to like that," she said.

The receptionist smiled. "Because I meet lovely people like you as well," she said. "What can I do to help?"

***

Jewel got off the lift on the second floor and looked up at the sign telling her which way to go for the ward and room number that she required. The corridor was long, and she could see a nurse in the distance holding what looked suspiciously like a bedpan. Jewel wrinkled her nose. This wasn't one of her favourite places. She would get in and see Jade then quickly get out of the place.

A trolley with the lunches followed her out of the lift and began to clank its way in the opposite direction. A smell of stale cabbage wafted out of the closed lids. Jewel winced. Hospital food wasn't what she considered gourmet fare.

As Jewel walked towards room 15, a staff lift opened in front of her and a stretcher emerged. A woman, eyes closed and waxen of face, with tubes oozing from various places on her body, was on it. The nurses were still covered in the blue surgical gowns, silly hats and slippers covering their extremities. None of them looked terribly interested in the patient or anything around them. No one apologised for interrupting her walk down the corridor.

Jewel looked the other way quickly. She felt like a peeping tom looking at the private parts of a complete stranger. She didn't much like that feeling.

She was relieved when she noticed that 'number 15' was above the entrance to the next room. She turned left into the spacious and light room. There were four beds. The closest, on the right, had an old white-haired lady in it. Her mouth was open, and she was snoring lightly.

To Jewel's left, a young girl was lying perfectly still. She had a white hospital blanket pulled up to her chin and a drip connected to her wrist. Her face was pale and gaunt. It took Jewel a couple of moments to realise this was her daughter. She stood at the foot of the bed and stared.

Jade didn't move.

"Jade." Jewel spoke quietly. She hadn't even looked at the other two beds.

Still Jade didn't move.

Jewel felt a tap on her shoulder. When she turned with a start, she was amazed to see a nurse. She hadn't heard her come in.

"Excuse me," the nurse said. "Are you a relative?"

Jewel nodded. "Yes," she replied abruptly, still speaking softly. "I'm her mother. "

"Aah," the nurse smiled. "I'll just go and get the senior nurse. I'm sure she'll want to talk to you." And she bustled out of the room and disappeared.

There was a chair next to Jade's bed. Jewel sank into it with a sudden despondency.

It seemed like hours that Jewel sat and just looked at her daughter. She was just beginning to feel fidgety, wanting to get back to work, when the senior nurse arrived. During the wait, Jade hadn't shown any sign of movement or awareness.

"Hello, Mrs Sutcliffe," the woman beckoned to her. "Would you follow me please."

Jewel got out of the chair with a touch of irritation and almost rolled her eyes at the dramatics, but just managed to control herself. She followed the rather plump woman out to the corridor.

The nurse turned to her. "They say that even in a coma, people can still hear."

Jewel nodded. She didn't really have anything to say. She stood still, face impassive, and looked at the senior nurse.

The nurse then added.

"Your daughter has suffered a brain injury and we have put her into an induced coma until the swelling goes down." She paused, waiting to see if this impeccably dressed and aloof woman would ask a question. When none were forth coming, she took a breath and continued.

"She was particularly aggressive when the paramedics picked her up after her fall and they had to sedate her. She had also reverted to the behaviour of a very young child. This is a symptom of brain injury and that was another reason to keep her sedated. The severity of this type of injury is difficult to judge so we don't know how long we will keep her in a coma, or how she will react when she comes out of it."

Jewel still hadn't shown any emotion, and the nurse was starting to feel uncomfortable. Jewel was waging a war with-in. Her fear for her daughter was immense, but she couldn't admit this to the nurse – a complete stranger. When it came apparent that the nurse was waiting for a comment, she blurted out.

"Well, I guess I'll get back to work."

The nurse raised her eyebrows.

"No use being here until she comes out of the coma. I'll ring later this evening and find out what progress has been made." She turned and walked down the corridor back to the lifts. The nurse stood, amazed at the attitude, before she, too, turned and made her way back to the nurses' station.

"Did you hear that?" she asked the duty nurse behind the counter. The nurse looked up and shook her head.

"What?"

The senior nurse clenched her teeth. "I've never seen anyone so cold and uncaring."

The nurse at the desk smiled. "It takes all types, Senior. Perhaps the worry has made her angry inside? You know how people can re-act to stress!"

"Yes, I guess so. You're right. I very nearly lost my cool and told her what I thought of her! Now I need a coffee! I'll settle in a minute – I just hope I'm not on duty when she comes again – 'cos I might not be able to hold my tongue next time."

The duty nurse smiled again.

"Honestly, Senior. I couldn't imagine *you* losing your cool!"

"I should hope not," the senior replied, then walked off to the staff room to get the much-needed coffee. At her desk, the nurse smiled as she watched the senior nurse disappear into the staff room, then she returned to her paperwork.

***

When Jewel got back to the real estate agency, David approached her.

"Everything OK?" he asked.

Jewel looked at him and shrugged slightly. "My daughter seems to have given herself quite a bump on the head. She's in a coma, so I'll ring later to see if there has been any improvement."

David reached out his hand to touch her, and Jewel drew back.

"Did you let the Forsyths know?"

"Yes, of course." David frowned. "They were most understanding."

"Good." Jewel responded. "I'll give them a ring and sort out a time in the next couple of days so we can look at that property. I think it's perfect for them." With that she went to her desk and picked up the phone.

David slowly turned and went back to his office. This was a side of Jewel he didn't particularly like. He couldn't relate this woman to the one he dated and had loved for some time. Admittedly, she had been a bit distant on occasion, but he had always thought that was a reaction to something he had done. Now he wondered if she was afraid to really let herself be vulnerable, if she had some hidden flaw that would cause him to be repelled. He had thought that there was a softer side hiding underneath the sophistication she worked so hard to maintain. He also knew that in bed she could be a tigress. He'd never been able to find out what had happened in her past to cause such a mask to be put in place.

Perhaps this accident with her daughter might be able to crumble some of the walls Jewel had built around herself.

If that were the result, David would be very happy with the outcome. He had been trying for months to soften her, with his gifts, with his understanding. Even at the height of their lovemaking, he had always felt a detachment from her that hurt his soul. He had thought that he wasn't trying hard enough, not giving enough of himself to the relationship. Now he wondered whether it would ever get any better, whether she was intrinsically selfish and really didn't consider his feelings at all.

He heard Jewel in the background of his thoughts, speaking on the phone. She had a light lilt to her voice, as if her daughter's predicament was of no importance to her. She spoke pleasantly and, when he really listened, a bit forcefully. She was in her element. She 'worked' the Forsyths until he heard her put the phone down.

She came and poked her head around the office door.

"I'm going out with the Forsyths now." David raised his head and looked over the top of the computer screen at her. She gave a brief laugh. "No point in missing out on a sale," she said, then he heard her heels click down the hall, the door open and shut, and she was gone.

4.

Topaz crept into the house at 3.00a.m. After her gig at *'The Blue Stocking'* nightclub, she had had a few drinks then gone to Gus's office. He'd closed the blinds, leered at her and grabbed her breasts. Then they'd had a quick tumble on the desk. Excited and sexually aroused, Gus had taken her quick and hard.

Now, as she took her shoes off and tiptoed along the hallway, she was feeling a bit sore and still a little drunk.

She didn't want to wake Saffy, and, even though the light on the answering machine was flashing, she staggered to her bedroom.

She undressed.

Looking at herself naked in the full-length mirror she noticed a bruise starting to appear around her right nipple. She spread her legs and used her fingers, but couldn't get an orgasm – she hadn't succeeded with Gus on that hard desk, while wondering if anyone would enter the office. Gus had been hoping they would be sprung – it gave him a thrill that they might. It had always given such an edge to sex in the past, but it wasn't working for her anymore.

As she thought of finding another man, a stranger watching her as she played, her body finally twitched into a shudder of pleasure, and she watched as Gus's residual sperm ran down her legs. She smelt her fingers, then licked them and grinned at the taste. At least Gus's sperm and her own juices had always tasted good! Then she collapsed in a fit of giggles on her bed. The room twirled for a while, and she lay with her legs open and throbbing. Finally she sank into a deep alcohol induced sleep.

***

It wasn't until about 10 o'clock the next morning when she finally opened her eyes. She was still on top of the covers, and she was cold. Her head ached and her eyes felt like they were full of grit. She rolled off the bed, grabbed her dressing gown and wrapped it around herself then made her way to the bathroom.

She had absolutely no desire to do anything. She tip-toed passed Saffy's room, fleetingly wondering why she hadn't heard her up and about, then made it to the kitchen and turned on the kettle. She looked at the toaster for a couple of moments, trying to focus her eyes, and decided that toast was beyond her at the moment.

She made a strong cup of coffee and went back to bed. She placed the coffee on the bedside table and snuggled back under the covers. She was asleep before the coffee had begun to cool.

***

At three o'clock in the afternoon, she turned and squinted at the clock.

"Christ – time I was at rehearsal!"

She vaulted out of bed, dashed to the toilet, brushed her hair and then threw on a pair of jeans and a lace blouse. She skipped down the hall to the front door still trying to get her second shoe on. As she passed the answering machine, she momentarily paused – but as she was late she continued on her way.

"I don't have time – I'll check it when I get home tonight."

When she reached the front door she yelled back up the hallway. "I'll see you when I get home Saff! Haven't got time now!"

Her high heels stuttered down the pathway like a baby machine gun. The garage door rose up at the touch of a button, she slid into the driver's seat and slammed the door. Then she backed the car out with a screech of tyres and was gone down the road before the clock had clicked over to 3.15.

***

Saffy crouched behind the large skipbin in the alleyway, trying not to look around the edge to see if she had been followed. She didn't think the waiter at the café had continued to chase her. Her heart was still beating a million miles an hour but she thought she was safe. When she heard the backdoor of the hardware shop open, she was sure whoever had come out would be able to hear the loud thumping of her heart.

She ducked down even further, trying to curl into a size as insignificant as possible. She closed her eyes and held her breath. The footsteps came closer. She felt the skipbin move, as whoever was there flung a cardboard box on the top. Then she heard the noise of a lighter being flicked several times, and the smell of smoke tickled her nose. She let out her breath slowly, then took it back in, as she felt the need to cough and then sneeze. She pressed her lips together very tightly, but the sneeze came anyway. She swallowed it, making a muffled grunt, and hoped she hadn't been heard. She thought a car going by at the end of the alley might have drowned out the sound, but she couldn't be sure. She sat still, waiting to be discovered.

Nothing happened.

She tried to think of something she could say that would explain why she was hiding where she was, but her brain was blank with fear.

She sat on.

Eventually she heard the door to the hardware shop squeak open and close and she thought she was alone. She couldn't hear anyone talking to whoever had come out into the alley, so she presumed that what she had heard was the person going back inside. She waited for a few more minutes, then cautiously stood up to look over the top of the bin.

No one was in sight.

She breathed again, taking in little hiccups as if she had been starving for air. She forced herself to calm down and breathe normally. She didn't want to hyperventilate right now. Once her breath was back to normal and her heartbeat wasn't thumping in her ears, she stood up completely. The alley, right through to the shops on the street, was blissfully empty.

Then, with head held high and no apparent rush, she walked out of the alleyway onto the pavement of the shopping centre. She turned away from the café she had tricked, and casually sauntered toward the main road. All the while she was alert and ready to run if need be.

She made it to the main road and turned left. She realised the sun was beginning to get fairly low in the sky, and that the shops were closing.

Another day was already coming to an end. So far she was free. No one had accosted her; no police had seen her. She knew she had to decide what to do next.

Ever since the accident, she had convinced herself that everyone was out to get her. When she had met Jade, she had been on medication for depression, and to find a friend with a name of a gem was amazing. Saffy hated that her mother had called her Sapphire; that the women in her family were all named after gems. Jade had been sympathetic. She explained that her family had done the same – used the same theme. They had laughed together.

She still couldn't believe that Jade was gone. Why had she turned her back on the prancing horse? Jade was the only friend she had ever had.

The state of Saffy's mind was once more plunging into irrationality.

Where would she go?

She still wasn't confident enough to go home, although she tried hard to remember if tonight was a rehearsal night or a performance night for her mother at '*The Blue Stocking*'. If it was a performance night, Topaz wouldn't be home until the early hours, and Saffy could get home, pack some things and be gone again before her mother even missed her. As long as her mother wasn't home.

That settled it in her mind. She *would* go home. It was a sensible idea. A good idea. If there were lights on at home it meant her mother was there, so she didn't have to go in. She could turn away, and nobody would be any the wiser. If Topaz wasn't home, she would be able to get some clean clothes and also have a feed.

She began the long walk home.

5.

The day after the accident Ruby was again sitting in front of the television, but she couldn't settle. She had struggled out of her chair at least three times and walked to the door and then went back and sat down again. She was still wondering how the girls from the park were. Jade and Saffy had been so young and she was worried about Jade.

She got up once more, almost tripping over Punch, who had been about to jump up on to her lap. She absently bent and patted him. His back arched and tail frizzed, but even he knew that her mind was elsewhere.

She went back once more and stood at the back door. She stared out at the unkempt backyard, and then opened the screen door. Punch dashed under the lounge. He wasn't going to be shut in the laundry again if he could help it. But Ruby sighed and shut the door and wandered back to her armchair.

With a loud grunt, she sank back, allowing the comfort of the chair to surround her and shut her eyes. Memories came flooding back.

***

In 1943 she'd been a gorgeous young girl of seventeen. The war raged around her, but she had felt safe. There were hushed rumours circulating about Jews being herded away, but this didn't concern the young Ruby. Nobody in the village really believed it.

She still remembered the day that had changed her life forever as if it were yesterday. The events of the day were carved into her mind like the wheel ruts of a car on a gravel driveway.

It had been a glorious day. The sun had been shining and her friends had suggested a picnic.

She had met her friends by the stream, and there, looking like a young God, she met Carl. He was an officer in the German army and Ruby fell in love almost instantly. It had been much later that she had discovered he was an SS officer – he had looked so young.

Carl was also ready and willing to cuddle and kiss, and soon they wandered away from the group and Ruby's heart fluttered with happiness. When Carl began to breathe heavily and place his hands inside her flimsy cotton dress, she hadn't stopped him. He ripped at the bodice, a heat in his eyes that Ruby didn't understand. Before too long the dress had gone, her knickers, too and Carl had lain in her arms. She realised she was naked, while he fumbled with his fly, pushing his trousers to his ankles. His shirt felt rough against her bare breasts, and she closed her eyes, feeling shy.

What happened next was beyond anything Ruby had experienced or even imagined. Joining a man in such a way was exhilarating. Ruby was sure this was not supposed to be something that she should be doing, let alone enjoying.

When it began to hurt, she tried to stop but the situation seemed to be out of her control. Carl grunted and just kept pushing in to her, harder and harder, ignoring her pleas, until he moaned and finally lay still. He rolled off of her.

Ruby suddenly felt embarrassed, and collected up her tattered clothing and tried to cover up. Carl stood up, pulling up his trousers and looking down at her with a nasty grin. Immediately the promise of the day was crushed. Carl was looking flushed and continued to have a depraved look in his eyes. Ruby's skin prickled with apprehension.

"So that is what it is like to have a young virgin and a filthy Jewess as well!" he smirked. "Now I can tell my superiors what whores you all are."

Ruby was horrified, but scrambled up and away, back to her friends. They looked at her with disgust on their faces. Carl followed her, still leaving his trousers unbuttoned. He used his hand to stroke himself and his flaccid penis soon began to stand again. He made a grab for one of her girlfriends but Helga lurched away. In the process her dress had been torn as well and her breast revealed. Everyone looked frightened. Carl spat on her breast, laughing as she wiped the spittle from her naked flesh. He turned, pulling himself with great glee. They tried not to watch, but he stopped at one point and grabbed Helga's face and put it down close to his penis.

"Look, you bitch," he commanded.

When she closed her eyes, he slapped her with his other hand. As she fell, he grabbed her hair and held her, so that his semen could spray all over her face. He tore the rest of Helga's bodice from her dress and wiped himself, throwing the material at Ruby with a grin. Then he growled, almost like an animal.

"You will be sorry you didn't all lie down and spread your legs for me. Next time I will bring my friends and you will do this. They would like to join in and watch such a thing." Then he strode off, laughing at their stunned and fearful faces. Ruby sat down next to Helga, who had burst into tears and tried to comfort her. Helga pushed her away.

"Did you know this man?" She asked.

"No. I thought he was your friend." Ruby looked around at the other girls. They were all whispering together and looking at the two girls as if they had become contagious with some rare and terrible disease.

"Did any of you bring him here?" Ruby asked, looking up at the now silent group.

The girls just shook their heads.

"I don't know where he came from." Trudi was full of courage *now*! She sneered at Ruby. "I thought he must have been *your* friend! He certainly knew that you would let him have his way with you! After that last exhibition with Helga, I am surprised he took *you* away out of our sight."

Ruby blushed. Now she knew she was soiled in their sight. At the time she hadn't realised that she was doing anything bad.

They quickly dispersed. The day had been spoilt. As she cycled home, she went over and over in her mind what she had let him do. She was mortified. She felt dirty and defiled by the experience, had lost her friends and would probably never see Carl again. She would have to hold the secret inside, and never tell a soul how she had allowed someone to take her virginity in such a way. Her parents would be cross, disappointed and ashamed and would probably punish her. Her decision made, she lowered her head and pedalled furiously, hoping that the exercise would make up for her slip from grace.

Two days later, there was a knock on the door.

The family was all in the kitchen getting ready to eat lunch. Ruby's mother spoke to her son.

"Please go and answer…." But before she had got any further, the door burst open, and Carl led several soldiers in to their home.

The soldiers rounded up her Mother, Father, two brothers and herself. Carl seemed to take pleasure in the fear that emanated from her family.

When her Father struggled, Carl ordered a soldier to shoot him. Her mother cried out, but the soldiers left the body on the floor, pushing the rest of the family out of the building and on to the street. There were several other families, including Helga's, cowering in a group next to a truck.

Carl barked some orders, and the canvas sides of the truck were thrown aside, and everyone was forced onto the back of it. Gun barrels poked several people when they hesitated, and two more men were shot. Several of the children began to cry, but the soldiers took no notice. They were even crueller, shouting, hitting and pushing until the whole group was up in the truck.

Then the truck started and they were on their way to who knew where. Everyone was silent, afraid to say or do anything. The mothers tried to quieten the younger children. The men looked silently angry that they had been so humiliated and not been able to look after their families. The teenagers looked scared. The wind whistling through the cracks of the sides was cold and the truck uncomfortable. The tarpaulin flapped and conversation, if they had been brave enough to talk, impossible. They were squashed together and used each other's bodies to give themselves some warmth and feeling of security.

The trip took three days.

They were given no food or water. Several of the old women fainted and soiled themselves with fear. The children wailed and some were sick. The lack of toilet facilities and the fact that the truck stopped only to change drivers meant they lost their dignity when nature called.

The men tried to be brave, but even they could do nothing. If one of them asked for some care they were just shot and pushed off the truck to lay where they had fallen.

Ruby wondered if this had been all her fault or maybe Helga's. At least she had given Carl what he had wanted. Perhaps he had told his superiors and they had decided to punish Helga and her for their actions. There was no way of knowing.

When they finally arrived at their destination the hushed rumours they had heard around their home now became truth. They were all forced off the truck. Anyone who couldn't walk was pushed out into the snow and the soldiers shot them. Then the soldiers asked the men from the truck to dig holes and put the bodies in them. They were forced, at gunpoint to bury their own loved ones.

When the trucks were behind the barbed wire of the camp, they were hustled out and made to shed their clothes. The soldiers turned on water hoses and ordered them to bathe; several soldiers hitting anyone who refused.

They were paraded in front of some sort of administrator and his colleagues, who were all dressed in thick uniforms and coats because of the cold.

The commandant poked at several women – feeling their breasts, looking in their mouths at their teeth and even asking a couple to bend over and then checking their back passages. He had looked over to the other men and pointed and laughed. It had been humiliating, standing in the nude before the other women and many strange men.

One man came over to a young woman, and with the commandant holding her down they checked her private parts. They took her away to the office, and she was never seen again, although they had been forced to stand, naked and shivering in the courtyard, listening to her screams. Finally, when silence once more descended, several soldiers came out of the office, adjusting their clothes, laughing and chattering.

They gathered the woman and children together like cattle and took them to one side of the camp. The men were taken to the another area.

They were herded into the huts – girls and children in one, women in another and the few men into another. The huts were bare and freezing. Mattresses were thin and there were very few blankets.

Ruby was glad when they were finally given some clothing, even though it wasn't their own. A small tin cup of liquid and a bowl of food were handed to each person. Both the liquid and the food were unrecognisable as anything she had known before. They were told to keep their utensils, as they wouldn't be given any more. Later, a young soldier came to the huts with a tattoo gun and marked a number on their arms.

***

Ruby shook her head. The memories had taken over and Punch was meowing at her to get him some food. She became aware that the room was getting dark, and she wondered how long she had sat there, remembering. She didn't like to recall the war, but, more and more of late, her mind was going back to the horror of those days.

She eased herself out of the chair and shuffled over to the cupboard, reached up and took out a tin.

"Goodness, Punch," she said to the cat winding around her legs, with its tail sticking straight up like the Eiffel tower. "You don't ever want to get so old. My knees hurt, my back is stiff." She glanced at the tin and sighed. She put the tin of baked beans back into the cupboard and exchanged it for cat food this time. "And my eyes are going! You, you rascal, all you can think about is food and sleep. You lucky thing."

Punch went over to the bowl she had placed on the floor and suspiciously smelled it.

"I haven't given you pickled onions, you know." She smiled. That cat had a personality all its own, and she loved it.

She decided that the tin of baked beans could be her dinner, so she took it back out of the cupboard, opened it and emptied it into a small saucepan. As it slowly heated, she made some toast. When it was ready she sat down to her meal, her plate on her knees. Punch watched her and decided that he would eat now too.

Finally she placed the empty plate on the floor and sat back into her armchair. Punch snuck around the back of the chair and licked the sauce off the plate until it almost shone. He jumped up onto the sofa and calmly licked his paws clean. Ruby went back to watching the television. She flicked through several channels until a documentary on the sea and its animals caught her eye. Her thoughts turned to Jade again for a moment, but she soon became more interested in the sharks and seals, and the girls and the accident slipped to the back of her mind.

6.

Not far away, Saffy was standing in the doorway of a solicitor's office. The little alcove created by the door was warmer than the pavement, and Saffy was beginning to feel cold. She wasn't far away from her home, but was having second thoughts about the wisdom of going back there.

She tried very hard to remember if her mother would be home, but eventually the cold of the night air penetrated, and she knew she needed to get some warmer clothes.

There were only a few shops open now. The local fish and chip shop looked warm and smelled of hot fat and sweaty bodies. The crowd around the door waited, stamping their feet and chatting loudly to each other as the cook over the deep fryers looked harassed and tired. Saffy sidled past.

On the corner, the pub was open and stank of stale beer and cigarette smoke. Several men were outside, arguing and jostling each other, their voices loud and uncouth. Saffy grimaced and tried to walk past them calmly.

One of the men moved towards her, and Saffy decided she wasn't staying there.

She ran.

Behind her she heard several of the youths whistle, jeer and swear at her. Saffy kept moving, not looking back.

She was lucky she wasn't far from home, so it didn't take much longer before she was walking up the driveway towards the garage. There were no lights on, and she breathed a sigh of relief.

Good.

Her mother was not home.

She located the spare key and let herself in. Without putting on the light she made her way to her bedroom. Her backpack was nestled behind the door. She grabbed it, went over to her wardrobe and thrust several different tops, another pair of jeans and some clean underwear into it. Then she put on a jacket, grabbed her backpack and dashed into the kitchen. She didn't want to be caught now.

Opening the fridge caused her to blink with the light and she quickly closed it again. No point in taking anything from there anyway. There were some tins of spaghetti in the cupboard and she stuffed a couple into her backpack and a couple of tins of tuna in her jean pockets.

At that point she heard a car and thought it might be her mother, so she made a dash past the lounge and headed to the back door. On the way she noticed the answering service light flashing, and thought it was probably the police trying to find her. She didn't hesitate. She was out of the back door and out of the yard, walking down the street as if she had a tiger on her tail.

***

Jewel arrived back from Point Piper long after David had closed the door at the office and gone home. She went home and collapsed, tired from the dramas of the day and the effort she'd made not to fall apart when she'd seen her daughter so pale and helpless in the hospital.

She rang the hospital several times the next day, but every time the nurse told her that Jade had still not come out of the coma. To stop the worry overtaking her, she spent the day working through her paperwork, ringing the Forsyth's and giving them more information.

David came into her office a couple of times during the day, but she smiled at him and told him there was no news. He left her to work, hoping she would let him know if Jade had awoken. At five o'clock he popped his head around the door.

"I'm going now – will you lock up?"

Jewel waved a well-manicured hand in his direction while she was on the phone, nodding to him as she did so. She was talking to the Forsyth's and David could hear the smile in her voice.

By the end of the day, she was almost sure that the Forsyth's were going to buy and she was feeling very pleased with herself. The future commission cheque was almost burning her fingers, and she longed to celebrate.

When she arrived home, she rang David on her mobile, her voice bright and burning.

"Hi," David answered the phone just as he was walking from the kitchen to the bathroom for a shower.

He was a little aggravated. He'd had a busy afternoon the previous day, after Jewel had gone to meet the Forsyth's. It didn't improve when Deborah, his receptionist, had also gone home. Debbie had been suffering with a migraine and David had let her go.

Today had been only marginally better. Debbie was still absent, and Jewel had been so wrapped up in the Forsyth sale, that he hadn't had a chance to relax.

Now, he was looking forward to a long hot cleansing shower, taking with it the dirt of the day's work. He almost hadn't bothered to answer the phone.

"Can I come over?" Jewel breathed into the phone, and before he could answer she added. "I've got a couple of bottles of red we can celebrate with."

"Oh? Why?" David was still peeved by her neglectful attitude to her daughter's accident and the fact she hadn't let him know what she was doing. "Shouldn't you be going to the hospital?" he said rather pointedly.

"Oh! I'll phone shortly and see if there's any improvement, but it's no use being there if she's still in a coma. I've rung several times – still no difference. Besides, I think we've made the sale on that million-dollar property at Point Piper. I feel like celebrating!"

David knew that Jewel would be ready for an aggressive and wild time in bed. Success always made her randy as hell.

He was tired. He hesitated. Maybe he should tell her not to come over. He thought about the sex. Damn! He was weak. He couldn't turn that down!

Jewel didn't even give him a choice.

"Never mind," she said. "I'll be there in about fifteen minutes." and the phone clicked.

David looked at the handset of his cordless and shook his head. When Jewel was in this type of mood, there was no stopping her. He wondered yet again if the relationship was ever really going to work. It was convenient, but he really didn't think there was any love on Jewel's side. He'd started out feeling that he would have a fling and it had surprised him when he had fallen in love with her. Now he was seeing quite a hard and cold side of her that he hadn't been willing to admit he had noticed before. The voice inside his head castigated him.

Oh yes you did, but you were enjoying the sex too much, weren't you?

He put down the phone, shaking his head with just a little bit of self-loathing and turned to go and have a shower.

He stopped. He picked up the phone again, found the local Chinese takeaway shop's number, pressed the number, and when there was an answer, ordered a feed for them – although he imagined it would have to wait until after they had satiated their lust for each other.

"Can you deliver in two hours?" he asked. "Good. Thanks."

He suddenly felt a little lighter, and began to imagine the next couple of hours with Jewel. By the time he got to the bathroom, he was already half erect.

He stepped into the shower and let the water run over his body, soothing the muscles and calming his mind. He thought about his wife. Alice had been so young and immature when they had married. Sex had been a shock for her and she had never got used to it.

It had finally destroyed their marriage. Since they had parted, David had overdosed on sex, picking up all kinds of women when he got the chance. Then he had landed the manager's job at the real estate where Jewel worked. When she had shown interest in him, he had been impressed. She was a beautiful woman, and when they had finally consummated their relationship, he had been amazed at the imagination, obsession and enjoyment she had displayed in sex.

He was still standing under the hot spray of the shower, when he heard the door open. He'd forgotten he had given Jewel a key.

Before he stepped out of the shower, she had stepped into the bathroom and was taking off her designer dress. She tossed it on the floor without a care and it pooled into a splash of colour on the tiles.

She opened the shower door and stepped in to David – still wearing a black lacy bit of nothing around her breasts and a tiny g-string pair of pants. She smiled and placed her hand between David's legs and started to caress him.

It didn't take long before David had divested Jewel of her garments, and carefully stepped out of the shower, lifted her off her feet and carried her to the bed. Water dripped across the carpet, but neither of them worried. The passion had overtaken all thoughts, and it took some control for David to remember to reach for a condom. Jewel laughed throatily and took the condom from him, put it into her mouth and softened it and moistened it, then placed it carefully over David's penis, using both her mouth and hands to stretch and mould it to his length.

David gasped – the whole operation was devastatingly sexy. He controlled the urge to push and come, because he knew she had so much more to give.

Jewel rolled over on to the bed and David began to explore her body, his hands and mouth finding all the sensitive areas that he knew she liked. When he reached the curls around the pink and swollen entrance to her core, he found the sensitive nub within her, and sucked it, gently biting until she squirmed and bucked.

She had licked and sucked him, too, but suddenly he felt her melt, and turned quickly, entering her sharply and with increasing pressure. He placed his hand between them, stroking her as he pulsed, and then pushed a finger of his other hand into her rear, pushing down with all his weight as he felt them both reach the point of no return.

She let out a groan, more of an animal snarl, and he felt the spasms inside clench his staff, bringing him to an even more satisfying climax.

They relaxed. He went to move, but she wouldn't allow him to leave her. He knew that within another ten minutes she would be ready again.

***

It was sometime later that the doorbell rang. David couldn't believe that they had been tangled together for two hours already.

"Don't answer it," Jewel moaned, still drunk with sex. She had got out of bed at one stage and brought in one of the bottles of red and drunk from the bottle, splashing some across her body for David to lick up. She was so uninhibited that she spread her legs and spread her vaginal lips with her hand and began to show him what she wanted. He licked her toes as he crawled from the bed.

"It's the takeaway," he murmured. "I'll get it and the other bottle of red and be back before you know it."

She continued to move, rubbing herself for him.

He grew tumescent again, flinging a towel around his waist and made it to the door.

As he left he grinned.

"I know just where I'm going to put some of the noodles, so I can eat them with your flavour," He suggested as he went to collect the food.

She shivered with pleasure.

***

When they finally lay spent and exhausted and too sore to carry on, the bottles of red empty and tossed on the floor, David thankfully slept. Jewel couldn't move, and the wine she had drunk had finally caught up with her.

A little later she heard David stir. She had no idea what the time was, but she wasn't going to move for any one. A voice penetrated the haze of alcohol and sex.

"Did you phone the hospital?" She opened her eyes a smidgen and looked at David with incomprehension.

David repeated.

"Did you check with the hospital and see how Jade is? You know – your daughter!"

Jewel mumbled and turned over.

"Jewel," he said again. "Your daughter. How is she? Have you even thought to find out?"

Jewel moaned.

"For God's sake, David," she groaned. "Leave it alone."

David lifted himself up onto his elbow and looked at her.

"Why don't you ring now?" he suggested.

"Nah, don't worry." She still hadn't opened her eyes properly and the vestiges of the alcohol and sex kept her brain irrational. "She'll be OK. She's just a drama queen. She's only got concussion, I think. If it was anything serious, they'd let me know."

David got up.

"Where're you going?" Jewel squinted at him.

"Well, I'm going to ring the hospital and find out." He was feeling cranky and guilty at not having the power to say no to Jewel, and his conscience was bothering him. He spoke with a growing impatience and irritation. "And I need to know that I haven't just fucked her mother into oblivion when you should have been more concerned about Jade."

He left her and went outside. She didn't move and he became angry.

When he looked at the clock, he realised it was two o'clock in the morning. Midnight shifts in the hospitals were notoriously short staffed. He decided to leave it till morning - Jewel was right. If Jade had come out of the coma, or deteriorated, they would have called. He realised calling in his half-drunken and angry state was probably not a good idea. He sighed, then strode back to bed.

Jewel was ready to take him again.

***

In the dark of the night, Saffy huddled in a doorway of a dingy little shop. She was frightened and cold, and the nightlife was keeping her awake.

She had seen a couple of men, almost too drunk to stand, urinate over each other as they passed out on the pavement. She had seen rats, cats and mangy dogs scurrying through the darkened streets, scavenging in bins and gutters. She had seen ladies of the night parading in front of slow moving cars until they had got money and joined the men. She had even seen one prostitute lift up her skirts to show an old man her naked genitals, and then let him take her, pushed up against the brickwork in a nearby alleyway.

She was amazed at these nightly going-ons that she had never known happened around her. OK, she knew there were drunks and prostitutes in the area, but she was normally curled up safely in a warm and comfortable bed. Her mother might be singing in a nightclub, but up until recently she had protected her daughter from the seamier side of nightlife in Sydney. She felt tears trickle down her cheeks as she realised she already missed the comfort of home.

Even in an extra pair of jeans and her jacket, she was still cold and miserable. She wished she had stuffed a small blanket in her backpack. She had not thought that she would feel so wretched and that the coldness of the night, a freezing and hard concrete slab beneath her as well as her numbing fear would have affected her so much.

She tried to sleep.

She must have dozed, because the next thing she knew, she was being kicked. She pushed herself further into the corner of the doorway.

"Hey, lovey." A man's voice slurred. "Can I have a fuck? I got five bucksh."

Saffy was so upset, she didn't hesitate. Jumping to her feet, she pushed at the man, who staggered and fell. She vaulted over the top of him and bolted down the road.

By the time she stopped, her heart was racing and her breath was hurting. She had no idea where she was and, in the dark, couldn't recognise any of the normally familiar landmarks.

A little further along the street, across the other side of the road, a light in a shop warmed the pavement with a dull glow. Saffy made her way over to it, carefully crossing the road after a taxi had slid past. She stared through the window at the inside of the shop. The steel grid through the glass protected the stock on display and she was aware she shouldn't touch it. If she did, she knew the alarm would bring the security here quickly. A clock on one of the walls told her it was ten past three in the morning.

The night had never felt so long. To make matters worse, she was hungry again. She had already eaten the measly rations from the tins she had grabbed earlier. She hadn't thought to grab any money from home, and she didn't have a credit card either. She began to sneak along the road, keeping in the shadows close to the shop fronts. It wasn't as if she was practised at being on the streets.

Down a side street, she saw a man come out of the back of a shop. The light spilled out, and she ducked back, not wanting to be seen. She carefully looked around the edge of the building.

She thought it must have been a bakery, as bakers had to work in the wee small hours to get their goods ready and fresh for the morning crowds. The man emptied a bucket load of something into the rubbish bin out the back. She could smell food. Her stomach grumbled loudly and she looked around in case anyone had heard.

The light dimmed as the man made his way back into the shop. Saffy stood still, wondering if she should go and see if there was anything she could eat. Maybe the baker would take pity on her and give her something nice.

She waited for some time before she crept along the alley towards the rear door. She could hear someone whistling inside.

The fear of capture tortured her. She took ages to get the courage up to make her way to the bin so she could look inside.

By moving around behind it, next to several cardboard boxes waiting to be crushed, she worked out she could quickly duck down and not be seen if the man came outside again.

Just as she stood to look into the garbage, a cat jumped out of nowhere and landed near her. It clambered up onto the edge of a steel rubbish can near the back door of the bakery, knocking the lid off. The noise as it clattered to the ground was deafening. Saffy shrieked and placed her hand over her mouth in despair at the sound. She scampered back into the shadows.

The whistling stopped and the man clumped over to the door.

"Piss off!" he shouted, waving his arms at the cat. The cat scurried off and the man went back to his floury bench.

Another cat came along to the overturned container, casually rummaged around in the mess, then sauntered away with something in its mouth. Saffy heard the baker mutter *'Bloody cats!'* but this time he stayed at his bench.

Saffy sighed with relief.

Her heart slowed to a steady beat now that she knew she was safe. Then reality hit. She couldn't believe that she was going to check a rubbish bin for food. She hadn't been on the streets for forty-eight hours, and she was already scavenging! She was disgusted with herself. She couldn't be that hungry.

She crept away.

***

Topaz got out of the car and made her way to the front door. She was tired and cranky. The rehearsal had not gone very well. Consequently she had gone through the whole set again, making her late. Now she had missed her favourite TV drama series. If she had known this was going to happen, she would have recorded it.

She reached over her head and pushed the button on her key ring and the automatic garage door slid shut. She unlocked the front door and walked in, flicking on the light as she did so. A noise alerted her, and she thought she heard the back door close.

She immediately froze. Who had that been?

She stood still and listened, but the house was silent again, except for a couple of minor creaks that made Topaz stiffen with apprehension.

With her heart in her mouth, she crept towards the kitchen. When she turned on the light, the empty room felt as if it was mocking her.

There was obviously no one in the house. Topaz decided to check on Saffy, and she went to her bedroom.

Saffy was not there. Her bed didn't look as if it had been slept in, but her cupboard doors were open, and several pieces of clothing spilled out onto the floor.

It seemed plausible to Topaz that Saffy had probably decided to meet someone or go to a party. She had not seen her daughter in three days, so she didn't know how long Saffy had been gone. Maybe there was a note somewhere.

"I really must have a talk to that girl! We don't communicate anymore like we used to last year."

The thought didn't last. She was too tired. She'd talk to her in the morning.

She checked the house again, but found nothing wrong, so she locked the doors and went to bed.

The answering service light still flashed.

***

When Jewel awoke next, the sun was well and truly up. David was nowhere in sight, and the room stank of red wine.

She felt terrible. Her head ached and her body hurt. Now, the 'high' of possible success was gone and the world took on a depressing note. Why she kept hurting David with her over the top sexual rampages, she didn't care to know. She rolled off the bed, hardly able to stand. Her undergarments were nowhere in sight, nor her beautiful 'Colette Dinnigan' dress that she had taken so long to save for.

She stumbled over the bottles as she made her way to the bathroom, noting with displeasure the red stains on both the bed and the carpet.

She crouched over the toilet, her breasts butted up to the cold ceramic of the bowl. She knelt on the tiles, put her fingers in the back of her throat and retched, but there was no result except for a sore throat. She glimpsed the mound of colour next to the bowl, and realised it was her dress.

She groaned.

She carefully stood, holding on to the towel rack to steady herself. Bending to pick up the dress caused her head to spin, and made her dizzy. She swayed a little, but managed to stay upright.

By the time the feeling had passed, she had noticed two scrunched up mounds of black in the shower recess. Those, she thought with a mental sigh, were her undies. They were soaking wet. She couldn't put those back on.

She tried to recall what had happened last night, but she knew she had once more 'sexed out' on the glory of expecting a sale. She was glad she had David – at least he loved her, and although she didn't want to admit it, she knew she was falling in love with him, too. She had tried so hard to keep her emotions under control since the hurt and heartbreak she had felt when everything had fallen apart with Jade's father. It was getting harder and harder these days. Jade's accident was already breaking down the barriers that she had spent years erecting.

Her mind descended into her life in her twenties. She fought to stop the memories, but they came unbidden and strong.

***

She had married Geoff when she had just turned twenty. Everything had been wonderful, even though her parents had not agreed and hadn't come to the wedding. Jewel had tried to reconcile with them, but to this day she hadn't been successful.

Then she had decided she wanted children, and Geoff had been horrified.

She had fallen pregnant anyway, and Geoff had hit her. "I don't want children!" he had screamed at her. "You tricked me!" It had been their first fight, and the bruises had hardly healed when it happened again. And again. Every time she didn't agree with his opinions, he gave her a hiding.

Somehow she hadn't lost the baby, and when she had finally had her little girl, Geoff had told her to keep the brat out of his sight.

From then onwards, the marriage had deteriorated rapidly, and when Jade had begun to toddle and Geoff had hit her for something so trivial Jewel couldn't remember what it had been, Jewel had decided to get out.

Unfortunately, by that time, she was frightened of Geoff's reaction to her requests that the only way out was to wait until he was at work and leave secretly.

She'd done it, too. It had taken her six months to get up the courage, and to squirrel away some money, but she had done it.

She'd finally escaped the abusive relationship and decided that it would never happen to her again.

She went out of her way to work hard, giving Jade the best that money could buy. She studied hard, obtained her certificate for the real estate business, and gone from strength to strength. Now she used men, just like she had been used. Well, at least, that was her intention. David's tenderness with her, and his patience when she became sexually aggressive, was cracking her tough exterior.

Of course, she knew men would never say no to good sex! And she prided herself on her ability to make any man beg for more, then not be able to perform as well as her. She had to admit she liked the feeling of power it gave her.

Damn it! She was OK! In her mind she was better than *any* man she knew! But still there was a niggling in her brain that maybe she was wrong. Maybe she was going to suffer for her selfishness. Then the niggle coalesced into a thought which she tried to silence. *But David is different.*

She shut her eyes, and pushed the thought away. Bending down very carefully, she picked up the dress and shook out the creases, then pulled the dress over her head. She needed to wait until the nausea settled, and then she walked out of the bathroom and out of David's flat. He could keep her knickers and bras until she needed him again.

When she arrived at the exit of David's building, she pushed the door slightly open then stood quite still watching the people walking by. Wouldn't it be wicked – to walk around without underwear on? Nobody would know, except her. She felt her vagina lubricate at the thought. She smirked with the feeling of the silk of the dress on her naked skin, and walked outside to her car.

***

Ruby awoke still sitting in the armchair in front of the television. She couldn't believe she had slept away the night in that position. A morning show was rattling on about the state of someone's kitchen and how much bacteria could be found in the fridge.

She tried to stretch, sending Punch to the floor. He yowled with indignation. Her lap, which had felt comfortably warm, now allowed the cold of the morning air to tickle her thighs. She shook slightly as she arose slowly, her old knees stiff and her back sore.

It wouldn't have been so bad, but she had been woken up by her dream.

She had dreamt about Rhoda.

She hadn't had that particular dream for weeks, although it was always close to the surface in every waking moment. Such a little girl to lose. Joseph and she had never been able to have children and Ruby mourned the loss of her only child.

And she still grieved.

***

When she had stopped shaking and shivering in the German camp, and a few weeks had passed, it had become apparent that she was pregnant.

In all the troubles that everyone had witnessed and experienced, this was not greeted with much dismay. Ruby told her mother about Carl, and it was merely assumed she had been raped. Ruby had been too ashamed to tell her mother that she had enjoyed it in the beginning, so she made sure she mentioned the torn dress, the shame of Helga and the spitting that Carl had done.

The words he had tossed over his shoulder were now seen to be a prophecy. Since that fateful day, here in the camp, she *had* been raped, even when her belly had been huge with child. Many of the women in the camp had also been used by the soldiers, to the jeers and cheers of many of the onlookers – other soldiers waiting their turn.

When her 'time' had arrived, she had been working in the fields, and the soldier kept poking her with his rifle to get her to do more work, even as the baby agonisingly slid out of her body. How the girl had survived, Ruby had never known. She had whimpered, then fallen silent. Ruby had carried her home, cuddled in her arms, her bloody dress still showing the stains of the afterbirth and the subsequent bleeding.

When the commandant had discovered the child, she had been placed in a separate hut and given extra milk.

"It is for the girl! Not for you! We must care for the child of our fatherland," the man said, as he believed it had been conceived by one of the soldiers at his camp. It could have even been his! He often came in to beat her if he heard the baby cry.

"You are being given special treatment, girl. Be grateful."

Ruby hadn't quite seen it that way, as she was still sent out to the fields to work, had not been given any new clothing and no more rations. She was under scrutiny all the time. The extra milk was for the infant – her breasts and body had been too weak to produce enough by itself.

One day a year later, when Rhoda had been toddling, Ruby returned from the fields to discover she was gone, and she was pushed back into the hut with the other women. She had never seen Rhoda again, and when she tried to ask the commandant, she had been put in solitary confinement for her trouble.

The years of the camp still burned in her mind. A lot of the men had disappeared and then some of the women and children. Year later she had found out that they had been taken to another so called 'death camp' further away and then gassed to death. Before help had arrived, the Germans had been exceptionally cruel, torturing many of the men and raping the women more often. In those last few horrible weeks, the Germans had finally realised that the war was lost. It was a small and pitiable band of people left at the camp when the allies had won the war and the prisoners had been released. The bodies of the prisoners were weak and they hadn't been given any decent food for months. It took years before the effects had faded, although for some it never did. The memories could flare back at the slightest provocation. No wonder her body had never let her fall pregnant again.

***

Ruby sat back down on the chair and stared at the TV. The screen flickered and her vision blurred. Some reporter was mentioning an accident of a Sudan Airways plane, with no survivors except a two-year-old boy. The newscaster sorrowfully declared that even he had just died from his injuries.

Ruby sat and drank her cup of tea. The world had not changed since the war. More wars were being fought than ever before, and people still died needlessly from tragic circumstances. Ruby just couldn't dredge up any sympathy anymore. Humans didn't seem capable of learning from the past.

Her mind drifted away from the gabble of the TV, and she thought of the injured girl she had helped. It didn't seem possible that is was only a couple of days ago.

She made a decision.

She would go to the hospital and find her.

See how she was.

Once again, she thought of Rhoda, and she hoped that someone had given her daughter the help and love that all children deserved, when she had not been able to do so. Without Ruby realising it, Jade had become a substitute for her daughter whom she had never had the chance to see grow up.

With aching joints, she once more struggled out of the embrace of the armchair, set down some food for Punch, changed into a clean dress and then put on a thick jacket. Punch eyed her with suspicion, but Ruby wasn't thinking of him. She left him in the kitchen, having forgotten he should have gone into the laundry. She plodded out of the back yard and made her way to the bus stop. The bus would take her to the train, which would then take her to the hospital in Darlinghurst.

7.

Jewel arrived at work a short while later. In the car, she had hastily put on some make-up to disguise the marks of her debauched night. She hadn't had time to go home and change. She was feeling slightly naughty at the lack of clothing under her dress. She wondered if David would notice.

David sat behind his desk; head in hands, feeling absolutely exhausted. He looked up as Jewel sashayed into the office.

"Oh my God," he groaned. "How do you do it! You look great – I feel like Hell."

Jewel smiled stiffly, her head high.

"What's the problem, hun?" she smirked. "If you can't take the heat … you know what they say!"

David just stared at the desk through his fingers. He knew that he would have a mess to clean up when he got home – new carpet would be needed as well as new sheets to buy. It had been an expensive night!

Jewel laughed, albeit a little harshly. She wondered how he'd feel if he knew she had no underwear under the dress. She almost showed him, but changed her mind. He looked completely whacked. She wasn't going to admit she also felt like she'd been run over by a bulldozer.

"Okay, Boss," she added. "Any prospects today? Have you heard from the Forsyths?"

When David shook his head, she twirled around and went to her desk. As she moved towards her room she spoke.

"Okay. I'll give them a call. Got to get the show on the road."

David just watched her – he didn't say a word.

Jewel walked into her office, closing the door behind her. She sat down at her desk and breathed heavily. It wasn't easy to keep up the façade.

After a couple of moments, she turned on the computer and then picked up the phone. Even pushing the buttons made her cringe, but she wasn't going to let it beat her.

David heard. *"Well hello, Gina."* said clearly and cheerfully through the wall, and knew Jewel was back on the job. He was amazed she was on first name basis with Mrs. Forsyth. Heaven help him if the sale went through and Jewel wanted to 'celebrate' again - and it sounded like it might – last night had nearly killed him!

His phone rang. He let out a soothing breath then picked up the handset.

"Hello, Moore Park Real Estate, David speaking."

He listened for a moment.

"Yes, I will tell her. Thank you very much."

He rose and made his way to Jewel's office, knocking on the closed door.

"Come in!" Jewel trilled, holding the phone away from her ear, hiding the throbbing headache she had, and the constant worry about her daughter.

David rolled his eyes with disbelief before he opened the door.

"Just had a phone call from the hospital. Your mobile must be off or out of charge – they couldn't get through to you. Lucky you'd left them your work number," he said. "Jade's come out of the coma, and they would like you to come in."

Jewel slumped a little. She said her goodbyes to Mrs Forsyth and put the phone back in its cradle.

"Damn – don't they understand I'm at work!"

When she saw the look on David's face, she grimaced.

"Okay! Okay! I'm going!" and she picked up her car keys and stood up. Her head throbbed and she felt a little faint. Playing the tough uncaring woman wasn't feeling right anymore. She took a deep breath as David watched, his forehead wrinkling in confusion, then she straightened her shoulders and walked up to him, caressing his chest and giving him a weak smile as she strode out of the office. Once outside and out of sight, she slumped with fatigue, screwed up her eyes as if to squeeze away the nausea that rushed up towards her throat, then almost sprinted to her car.

***

When she arrived at the hospital she parked the car, annoyed by the fee in a carpark she considered should be free, and made her way straight up to Jade's room.

She glanced at Jade. Her daughter was still, eyes closed. An old lady sat on the chair next to Jade's bed.

"Who are you?" she asked somewhat haughtily.

The old lady tried to rise, holding on to the wall for support.

She spoke quietly. "I'm Ruby," she answered. "Jade's sleeping. I was the one who helped when she had the fall."

"Oh!" Jewel felt a little uncomfortable with her attitude towards the woman, and didn't know what to say. She was saved from commenting when Jade opened her eyes.

Jewel moved across to the bed.

"Hello, Honey," she said softly. "How are you?"

Jade looked at her blankly.

"I want my Mummy," she said in a whisper.

"That's me, dear." Jewel clenched her teeth in an effort to stay sympathetic without giving in to the worry and surging anger inside. That this had happened to her little girl was so unfair. Her night with David had made her head hurt, and her whole body ache. She was so tired she couldn't think straight. "Don't be silly. I'm here."

A nurse bustled into the room. It was a different woman to the senior nurse she had spoken to before.

"Of course," Jewel thought with irritation, *"It's a different shift. Now I'll have to hear all the details again! Damn!"* At this point, all she wanted was to sit with Jade, relax with Ruby and hear what had happened and hope that her daughter would get better quickly. The accident was still not clear in her mind. She thought of Saffy as well and wondered where she was. She hoped Topaz was giving her lots of cuddles. Knowing Saffy the way she did, Saffy was likely to over react – she had a history of doing that. After all, Saffy had gone down into deep depression at the last school, when her best friend had died from a rare form of cancer. Saffy had felt like it had been her fault that her friend had become sick. The change of school, the friendship with Jade and a regime of tablets had made a huge difference. Now this accident with Jade may have slipped her over the edge again.

This had become complicated. She shut her eyes against the red haze of pain from the thumping in her head. The harsh light from the windows of the ward speared in behind her eyelids – so she opened them again. If only this was over, and she had Jade back. She silently promised herself that she would change, become a more understanding parent, a more compassionate human being. It almost made her smile as she thought that David would like that.

She looked at the nurse. The woman was frightfully bright and breezy for a nurse on this ward.

"And how are we coming along?" she said to Jade, holding her wrist while she took her pulse and ignoring Jewel and Ruby. Jade looked at her with incomprehension. The nurse checked the water jug, the drip line and the urine bag next to the bed, then wrote on the report hanging at the end of the bed.

"Try and drink up, there's a good girl." And then she whirled off to the next patient.

Jewel was left standing with her mouth open in astonishment. She looked at Ruby and lifted an eyebrow.

"Excuse me!" she said. "Can I speak to someone in charge?"

The nurse turned and gave Jewel a huge smile.

"Righto!" she said. "I won't be a moment. I'll just check the rest of the patients and then I'll get the Senior Nurse."

Jewel was about to tell the nurse just what she thought of her, when Ruby patted her shoulder and turned her towards Jade. Jade's eyes were large and tearful. She said "Mum?" in a quivery little voice, and Jewel melted inside.

It was a long time since she had had the rush of love for her daughter that had suddenly overwhelmed her. Her love for her daughter had been underneath all she had done, but now Jade's face looked so vulnerable, she felt emotion well up in her throat. She swallowed. Her voice came out a little brittle.

"Yes, love," she said and went to the bed and held Jade's hand. Ruby quietly slid out of the room, leaving the seat free for Jewel to use. It was about time she had a cup of coffee, so she made her way along the corridor and down to the cafeteria. She was glad Jade's mother had come to the hospital.

Jewel didn't even notice that Ruby had gone.

***

While Jewel was at the hospital, Saffy was walking along George Street in the city centre, clutching her backpack and munching on a bag of donuts that she had lifted from a shelf in one of the little bakeries. She was amazed it had been so easy. She had merely waited until the shopkeeper was serving another customer, then quietly shifted it from the shelf to under her jacket. When another assistant had asked her what she wanted, she had just waved her hand in the air and said she was just looking. Then she had walked out, trying hard not to rush or look guilty.

The donuts tasted better for the taking, although Saffy was exhausted by her experiences during the night. She had not slept well, and she was hoping to find a nice spot in a park somewhere, where she could curl up on the grass under the shade of a tree and have a reasonably good sleep.

She hadn't been game enough to approach any of the people she had seen in the streets last night, and she was still wary of everyone. She still thought she had nearly been caught at home. The light had come on in the hallway just as she had slipped out the back door.

Now, as she walked, her mind began to remember things that she had seen on television and always scoffed at. There had been documentaries about 'the homeless' who wandered the streets and how different organisations were there to help. When Saffy had been in the comfort of her own home she had thought the people on the streets were pathetic, and had only themselves to blame for their predicaments. If they just tried, they would be in a warm home and not be taking charity.

Now she felt differently. Yes, sure, it was her fault she was on the streets, but now all she wanted was a safe haven to sleep in, to get a free meal without stealing, and to meet people who cared.

She vaguely remembered that there was a Sydney mission that helped. She also thought that one of the churches had people that drove around at night and picked up drunks. She knew the Salvation Army were good people that could be relied on as well.

The problem was finding these people.

She finished the donuts and saw the entrance to Central Station. She needed the toilets, so she went in and used the moment to change into some clean undies and another top. Her jeans were still reasonably clean. She washed her undies in the sink, and scrunched them up into her backpack. Next time she was in a shop, she'd grab a plastic bag so they wouldn't wet the rest of her clothes. When she found a place to sleep, she would hang them up so they could dry.

Perhaps she could come back to the station tonight if she hadn't found the refuge. She could always go to a church, too. They were supposed to give people sanctuary.

By the time night was approaching, Saffy had managed to sneak another couple of apples from a greengrocer's display, but she hadn't found the mission place or any government office open anywhere that could help her. Not that she would have gone into one if she had found it. She was still too wary in case they had been warned about her and her circumstances had made her so paranoid that now any authority figure scared her.

She wasn't sure what to do next. Once again exhaustion and cold made her decide to look for shelter. It would be wonderful if she could find a place that would feed her as well.

She searched the city skyline and caught a glimpse of a church cross on top of a spire. It didn't seem to be too far away. She decided to make her way towards it hoping it was just around the corner. She trudged on, keeping her eye on the occasional glimpse of the spire in between the buildings. When she finally found it, she could have wept. The doors were closed and locked.

As she stood looking at the building with dismay, a boy came up and stood next to her. He was about twenty centimetres taller than her, and he had a backpack slung over one shoulder. His hair was tangled, and his face was dirty. He looked at her with sly brown eyes.

"You okay?"

Saffy stepped back ready to run again.

The boy put out his hand and touched her arm.

"Hey, she'll be right, kid! I won't hurt ya'."

Saffy didn't relax. She narrowed her eyes, and snorted.

"Yeah, right!" She no longer trusted anyone.

The boy's eyes crinkled with amusement.

"M' name's Rod," he said. "You look as if you could use a meal."

Saffy just stood and glared at him.

Understanding flashed across the boy's scruffy face.

"Oh! I bet you thought you'd be able to sneak into the church and sleep," he said. "These days the churches lock their doors – too much vandalism, I guess."

Saffy hadn't thought of that. Again she just stared, but stayed silent.

Rod spoke again.

"If you want, you can come with me. I know a place where we can get a good meal, and a nice warm place to sleep."

With that he simply swivelled on his heels and began to walk away. Saffy fought the doubts and worries for a couple of moments then followed him. She still wasn't sure if she was doing the right thing, but he was the first person who had spoken to her since the incident with her friend, and the only person who had given her some hope.

Rod stopped and looked at her.

"Great, kid, be suspicious. I'm not worried." He began to move away slowly. "Come on. Ya won't be sorry." He smiled and his face became almost handsome. "Anyhow. What's yer name?"

"Saffy," she said, then bit her lip – perhaps she shouldn't have given him her real name! She didn't know anything about him. Maybe Rod wasn't *his* real name.

He grinned. "Well, hi Saffy! Nice to meet ya." He put out his hand to shake hers, bowing in a parody of introduction.

Saffy stifled a giggle.

Then Rod held out his hand and gestured like robot number five in the movie '*Short Circuit*' – "Yo! Baby. Let's go!" and he strode off. Saffy had to run to keep up with him.

8.

Ruby sat in the hospital cafeteria and stared at the wall, her coffee in front of her untouched. Seeing Jade and her mother had triggered her memory once again.

She thought about the daughter who she had never had the opportunity to know. What had happened to the poor little girl? Did the Germans kill her? Somehow she didn't think so – surely she would have known. After all, they had given her the extra milk for her daughter. Why would they have done that just to get rid of her later? No, Rhoda was alive somewhere. She had to believe that. The other option was just too painful.

Had a German family adopted her? Had she been sent to another camp? Had she been part of the horrible experiments by Dr. Mengele? NO!! Ruby would *never* ever think that. When she had found out later about the atrocities that had happened in the other camps during the war she had been horrified. It had been bad enough where she had been, but there were worse elsewhere.

For a long while she had hated the Germans, but now that she was older and the past was so long ago, she had mellowed. The young people of Germany today were not to blame. In fact, many of the Germans she had met since had also been ashamed and disgusted.

War in any country was marred by horrible inhumane acts – that was what war brought out in some people. Even without the trappings of war, some people were just plain cruel. Why anyone would be like that or want war was incomprehensible to Ruby.

Now she sat and wondered. She glanced at the ceiling, as if she could see through the layers of cement up to the floor where Jade slept.

She had finally been able to find it in her heart to feel sympathy for the girl upstairs. Jade's eyes had reminded her so much of Rhoda.

The coffee was almost cold when Ruby finally drank it. It didn't matter. She had only left Jade's side in order to give the mother some private time.

The lift took her back up to the ward and when she arrived at room seven, she crept around the corner. Jade's mother was still there, holding Jade's hand and looking puzzled. Ruby thought it was wise to leave her alone.

She retreated and made her way down to the ground floor and then to the bus stop. She would come again tomorrow and see Jade, if she was able.

***

Topaz opened her eyes and stretched. Today was a free day, and after the lousy rehearsal yesterday she was looking forward to a lazy day.

"*I must have a chat with Saff today*," she decided, but there was no urgency in the thought.

She wrapped her dressing gown around herself, put on her slippers and sauntered down to the kitchen for some breakfast. As she passed Saffy's room she noticed that the bed still hadn't been slept in. She frowned. It wasn't like her daughter to stay out so long without leaving a message.

"*Aah!*" Topaz realised. "*That's why the message machine is flashing!*"

She took a detour to the hallway, and switched the messages onto the loudspeaker.

"Hi, Saffy. " a male voice said. "It's Brad here. I took the horses back to the stables. Are you at the hospital with Jade? Give me a ring when you get back."

Topaz looked at the message machine as if it had tried to stab her. How long ago had that message been recorded? She looked at the date. Two days ago!

So much for a lazy day. She should get over to the hospital. What had happened? Was Jade badly hurt? Was Saffy hurt? Which hospital? What was the time? Why hadn't Saffy let her know?

"Oh my goodness, why didn't I listen to the message before!"

Topaz raced back into her bedroom. No time for breakfast now. She looked at the clock. It was already 10.30 a.m. With trembling hands she dressed in a skirt and warm top.

Once she was ready to go, she tried ringing Saffy's mobile, but cringed when she heard it ringing in her daughter's bedroom. The ringing stopped. Saffy never went anywhere without her phone! She went into the bedroom. It was in the middle of the bed. Why hadn't she noticed it before? She picked it up, but the battery must have just died. She threw it, impatiently, back on the bed.

Now she was really worried.

By the time she slid behind the wheel of her car, her heart was pounding. She sat for a few minutes and calmed down. It wouldn't help Saffy, or her friend Jade, if she was a screaming mess or had an accident in her rush to get to the hospital. She didn't even know which hospital she was supposed to be going to.

She took another deep breath.

Eventually the blood stopped thundering around in her head and she began to think more logically. She would go back inside and ring several hospitals and find out as much as she could before she did anything stupid.

She got out of the car and walked inside. Taking the cordless phone into the kitchen, she sat on a stool, opened the phone book's Yellow Pages at 'hospitals' and began her search.

It was the third hospital she called that told her that Jade was in ward seven. When Topaz had explained her connection to the patient and her worry about her daughter, the receptionist said she couldn't find any mention that a Sapphire Brown had been admitted.

Topaz breathed a sigh of relief.

Then her voice in her head questioned – *"Where is Saffy?"*

"It's OK," the little voice answered. *"Of course. She'll be visiting Jade if it's visiting hours."*

There was immediate relief with that thought.

"Thank you." She said happily to the receptionist. Then she added "What time are visiting hours?"

When she returned to the car to drive to the hospital and visit her daughter's best friend, she was much calmer. She expected to find Saffy with Jade, and, although the receptionist couldn't discuss the patient's condition, Topaz, who never thought along the lines of a worst scenario, didn't think it would be too bad.

***

Jewel had hardly moved. She sat holding Jade's hand. The condition of her daughter had shaken her. She hadn't even thought of work since she had witnessed the state of her daughter's mind. She could see the blankness in Jade's eyes, and the fact that she had spoken in a tiny voice, like a three-year-old, was disconcerting.

"Mummy? When was the last time my daughter had called me that?"

She wanted to speak to the old lady who had been sitting in this very chair when she had arrived, but the woman had disappeared and not come back. Hopefully Saffy would know what had happened.

Jewel frowned. She had tried to contact Jade's best friend, but the girl hadn't bothered to answer her calls. This didn't make sense. The two were always together, in school and afterwards. They were the best of friends and did absolutely everything together.

Hopefully Saffy would come in soon and visit. She had a long list of questions to ask Saffy. Maybe she would get some answers.

Jewel spoke to Jade again.

"Honey, are you awake?"

Jade forced her eyes open as if each eyelid was weighted down with bricks.

"How do you feel?" Jade hadn't spoken again since her tremulous query when Jewel had first arrived. She didn't speak now, either.

Jewel rubbed her hand.

"Come on, Honey. Get better," she said softly. "I don't know what I would do if I didn't have you."

A smile fluttered across Jade's face, and Jewel was thrilled. Somewhere inside this gaunt teenager was her feisty Jade. But this time, it didn't emerge. Jade's thumb went back into her mouth, her eyes closed and she drifted back to sleep once more.

Jewel got up and stretched her legs. Her back ached and her mind was in turmoil. What should she do now? She suddenly thought of David.

"I'd better let him know what's going on, or he'll never forgive me!"

She took one last look at her daughter then walked out into the corridor.

A nurse came towards her, walking next to a male. The man saw Jewel and spoke to the nurse. They parted company and he came towards Jewel.

"Excuse me, Mrs Sutcliffe?"

Jewel stopped.

"Yes? Ms. Sutcliffe, actually."

"Nice to meet you," the young man said. "I'm Jade's doctor – Doctor Rogers. I wonder whether you have a moment so we can have a chat?" His eyebrows lifted as he asked the question, and Jewel looked at him a little closer. She had thought he was too young to be a doctor, but on second sight, she noticed the beginnings of wrinkles, and the few strands of grey at the temples.

"Certainly," she agreed.

"Come with me to the consulting room," he said. "I'd like to talk to you in private. It's just along here."

He stepped aside and placed his hand at her back to guide her towards a door about four metres further up the corridor.

He opened the door, gestured towards a seat where she could sit, and sat down himself.

. The doctor told her that Jade had regressed to her childhood, and they didn't know if or when she would get back to normal. Jewel was shocked. The conversation was hard to accept

"But didn't she just bump her head? Isn't it only concussion?"

The doctor showed great concern and patience.

"Yes and yes," he said "But the bump was severe, and the brain has swollen. We kept her in the coma until the swelling had gone down, but there is also bruising on the brain, and we will have to wait and see just what damage that may have caused."

Jewel was stunned. There was no way she had thought this was possible.

"How long before we know?" she asked, aware that she didn't really want to know the answer if it wasn't good.

The doctor's smile was caring and soft.

"We don't know," he said. "But I have to tell you, that your presence and love is very important. You should keep talking to her and reassuring her."

The real estate office and her job paled into insignificance compared to this situation. Even though Jewel gave the appearance of being selfish and only interested in money, the truth of the matter was that she was working so hard so she could put herself and Jade into a safer financial position. If Jade wasn't part of the equation, Jewel didn't want to examine her motives too closely, because she had a sneaking suspicion that the appearance that she gave out to the world just might be all there was.

"From now on, I must think of Jade more. What if she is permanently disabled? How would I cope? Oh my God, I can't face this. I don't know what to do? I'm scared of mental problems. It can't happen to my *daughter. I will be so embarrassed."*

The thoughts continued running around inside her head, while the doctor looked at her searchingly. She felt the warmth of a blush rise across her face. She was ashamed of herself that she should think such things. She hoped she hadn't actually said any of these thoughts out aloud. She wasn't sure, because the next thing the doctor said made her redden even more.

"I know this is a hard thing to hear," he commented. "And I realise that most people are afraid of mental illness, but really, Jade may pull out of this with very little damage."

Jewel tried not to let a breath of relief escape. Then the doctor went on.

"When your daughter is finally well enough to go home, she will be under observation by the head injury section of your local hospital for a further twelve months."

"Oh." Jewel was still too overwhelmed to say more.

The doctor continued. "In the meantime, we will be keeping a close watch while she is here. We trust that you will be able to continue to be able to look after her once she leaves the hospital? She will need constant supervision for some time."

The last was said with a raise in his voice and he stopped and looked at her, waiting for a reply.

"Um," Jewel looked thoughtful. The doctor waited.

Finally Jewel said. "I will have to work out something."

The doctor nodded. "Yes, I'm sure this has come as something of a shock right now. It will be an enormous commitment if Jade doesn't recover as we would like."

It wasn't long before the doctor was ushering Jewel out of the room. She was still in a daze, and couldn't remember what the last things were that the doctor had explained to her.

She made her way back to Jade's bedside, and the doctor came, too. The doctor stopped at the nurses' station and began a meeting with them. Jewel continued on, sat down heavily on the chair next to the bed and stared dejectedly at her daughter.

She had forgotten to ring David.

***

Meanwhile, Topaz sat in her car, drumming her fingers on the steering wheel. The traffic was crawling along at a snail's pace, and Topaz was getting impatient.

She wished she hadn't taken this particular road, but she hadn't known about the road works several metres in front of her. The workmen were only allowing a few cars at a time to pass, and Topaz was getting more and more stressed.

A motorcycle weaved its way past her and reached the front of the queue, but the signal went red and he was forced to stop. Then the workmen waved on the oncoming traffic, and Topaz grinned inside.

"Serve him right!" she thought. *"That'll teach him to try and beat the queue."*

When they were moved on again, Topaz realised she had missed the turning to the hospital. It didn't help her mood! She had to drive another kilometre before she could find the opportunity to turn around.

Consequently, by the time she drew up in the hospital car park and parked the car she was angry with frustration. She got out of the car and slammed the car door with some ferocity. It caught the cream cashmere top she had put on, and ripped a hole in the material. She raised her eyes to heaven and took a deep breath. Nothing was going her way today!

When she arrived at the entrance of the hospital she stopped and looked at the magazines in the shop that sold everything from candy to puzzle books for visitors to take up to the patients. She wasn't going to buy anything, but she needed to give herself some time to calm down. She wasn't going up to see Jade while she was so frustrated and worried. Hopefully Saffy would be there as well.

After a little while she felt better and made her way to the reception area.

The lady behind the counter was busy on the computer.

"Be with you in a moment'" she said distractedly, not taking her eyes off the screen.

Topaz waited.

The woman finally asked Topaz if she could help.

"I wonder whether you could let me know which room Jade Sutcliffe is in?" Topaz smiled brightly.

The receptionist looked back at the screen for a few moments.

"Sorry," she said. "Miss Sutcliffe is in no condition to see visitors. The doctor has put a 'family only' note here just in the last couple of hours. Are you a relative?"

"No condition? My goodness, what happened?"

"Are you a relative?" the receptionist asked again. "Because we have no authority to let out that type of information."

Topaz hesitated. She was tempted to lie, but she said. "No! I'm the mother of the girl who was with her when she had the accident."

"Oh, sorry," the woman behind the desk said. "I'll try and see if I can let you up there, if you would like?"

Topaz nodded. "I would really appreciate it. I was hoping my daughter was up there with her at the moment, but as the doctor only wants family to visit, I guess she isn't. Has she been in already?"

The woman grabbed the phone on the desk and spoke for a few moments. When she turned back she shook her head.

"Sorry," she confirmed. "The doctor doesn't want any one other than family there at present. He did say that only the mother is up there, although an older lady visited earlier. There have been no other visitors."

Topaz frowned. Who was the older lady? Maybe Jade's grandmother? Where was Sapphire?

Distractedly she turned away from the desk. "Thanks," she mumbled as she made her way back to the entrance. Where should she look now? Who would be able to answer her questions?

She was back at the car park before she decided she should try the real estate agent where Jade's mother worked. She didn't have anyone's phone numbers, as she had actually only met Jade's mother once or twice, but she knew she worked in Moore Park. It couldn't be too difficult to find a real estate agent there.

She sat down in the driver's seat of her car and reached over and took the map from the glove-box.

She traced the route with a manicured finger, then started the car and was on her way.

9.

Rod strode ahead of Saffy, not looking back. She followed at a distance, not wanting to appear too interested or, in fact, too desperate. She had begun to run, but slowed down, feeling that it made her look undignified, and for some reason, she wanted to make a good impression on Rod.

Several minutes later, Rod turned into the next street and for a moment, Saffy lost sight of him.

When she reached the corner she was hoping against hope that she would still be able to see him.

She turned, and there was Rod, only two metres away, leaning on the fence. His arms were folded and his ankles were crossed.

"You really want to come, or are you a lost cause?" Rod drawled. "I'm not going to spend my time waiting for you – either you get a move on, or I'll leave you here!"

Saffy very nearly told him where to go – but she stopped, took a breath and said. "OK!" Her face took on a sullen look. She glared at Rod.

"OK! OK!" she spoke a little louder. "Don't get yer knickers in a twist – I'm coming!"

Rod smirked "Right!"

Then he took off again, striding even more purposely. Saffy stopped and stamped her foot. This time she lost it!

"Stop, you bastard!" She shouted. "Don't go so fast!" Rod didn't turn. He merely shortened his steps. Saffy wasn't impressed.

"OK!" she yelled. "If you don't want me to come, you can go to Hell!"

Rod stopped. He turned and looked at her with a grin on his face.

"That's more like it!" he laughed. "Now I can see a bit of fighting spirit!"

He waited.

She waited.

After a few seconds, she caved. She walked up to him and said, with a scowl. "Well, come on. Let's go!"

Five minutes later Rod pushed open a door. It led into a corridor, then up a flight of steps. At the top was a large, bright room, with mirrors down one side, and bars along the wall to hold onto. It was obviously a ballet studio.

Saffy was confused.

Rod smiled. "This is my joint − well, at least − it is at the moment," he explained. "I used to be on the streets not so long ago."

Saffy looked bewildered and puzzled as her eyes circled the studio.

Rod continued. "I could see myself in you when you were outside that church. Someone helped me and everything got better from that moment for me, so now I'll do what I can for you. Sort of like a payback!"

"Why me?" Saffy looked at him with some suspicion. "I don't think you can help me. You don't know what I've done!"

"It doesn't matter." Rod shrugged. "We'll eat − you can get some sleep and then you can make up your mind if you want to stay or go!"

He opened a door in the back wall, and it led into a small kitchen. He opened a cupboard and took out some pasta and a tin of bolognaise sauce.

"This'll do," he murmured, grabbing a saucepan and turning on a hot plate on the small stove. He popped a couple of slices of bread in the toaster and set some water to boil in order to cook the pasta. Saffy didn't take her eyes off of him. She watched every movement with impatience. Finally he emptied the can of bolognaise sauce into another saucepan. As it warmed, the tantalising smell filled the room, and Saffy felt her mouth fill with saliva. She hadn't realised she was so hungry.

When they had both eaten, Rod led them back into the larger room. In the corner were some beanbags. Saffy flopped down on one, her stomach replete and her eyes nearly closed. Rod didn't speak. He grabbed the blanket that was scrunched up on the beanbag next to Saffy and flung it to her. She wrapped it around herself, wriggling around until she was comfortable.

He went to the other end of the studio and disappeared behind a small wall that Saffy hadn't noticed before. She heard the toilet flush, then Rod came back, another blanket in his arms. He sat down on the other beanbag, wrapped himself in the blanket and turned his back to her as he snuggled down.

Before too long they were both asleep.

***

About four o'clock in the afternoon, Jewel wiped her eyes. The tears for her daughter had come unbidden, and she had sat for hours next to the bed. Jade slept on, and Jewel finally came to the conclusion that it was time she went home.

The woman who left the hospital that day didn't bear any resemblance to the one who had blustered her way in earlier that morning. The duty nurse watched her drag one foot in front of the other, and shook her head. The senior nurse, who had complained about her attitude that first day, was back on duty, and as they stood next to one another, she said to the duty nurse.

"I wasn't expecting that! Maybe we misjudged the woman. Quite often people cover worry with anger, humour or arrogance" she cocked her head towards the departing Jewel. "It must have hit her pretty hard when she understood the ramifications of her daughter's injury."

The duty nurse replied. "Mmm. I guess so. She didn't moved from the chair next to the bed after Doctor Rogers spoke to her earlier. She held her daughter's hand for a long time, just watching her."

Jewel stepped into the lift and disappeared from view and the nurses returned to their duties – one to the ward and the other to her office.

When the lift reached the ground floor, Jewel watched dazedly as the doors opened. A man entered.

"Hello, Jewel," he said.

She came to with a jerk and saw David.

He was staring at her.

"Are you alright?" he asked, looking at her with a puzzled frown. "How's Jade?"

"Oh, David," Jewel flung herself into his arms. David's arms went around her in an automatic hug, but he was surprised.

He was stunned to realise that Jewel was sobbing into his chest. He stood in the lift, perfectly still, as the doors closed and the lift began to rise again.

"It's OK!" he murmured over and over again, patting her and hugging her tightly. This wasn't like Jewel. David had never seen her this vulnerable. It was eye opening for him and he liked what he saw. He kept his arms around her until the sobbing eased.

She stepped back a little, but not far enough away to lose the contact with his chest.

"I'm sorry," she spoke into his sweater and the sound was muffled.

The doors of the lift opened and they were on the fourth floor. David pressed the 'ground' button and the doors closed again and the lift descended.

David stood with his arms around a still quietly weeping Jewel, as the lift stopped at each floor, eating and disgorging nurses, doctors, visitors and, at one point, a Pink Lady with her trolley of magazines and little treats for patients who hadn't received any visitors.

Jewel never noticed. David never moved.

When the lift reached the ground floor again, he gently guided Jewel out of the lift. She looked around the foyer with red eyes and a dazed look. Without a word, he manoeuvred her further, to a table and chairs in a small coffee lounge set up for the comfort of visitors and patients alike.

She sat.

David spoke. "Stay there, I won't be long. I'll order a cappuccino for both of us. You look as if you need it!" He stroked her back in a comforting gesture as he moved away. She watched him go to the counter and saw his lips move. Everything had gone pear shaped in her life and she couldn't have moved even if she had wanted to.

It was only a couple of minutes later, and David was sitting opposite her.

He reached for her hand, and looked deep into her eyes.

"Tell me."

Jewel shook a little, and she whispered. "Jade."

David nodded with understanding. "Mmm. I was coming to get you. I spoke to reception and they said no visitors except family. I lied and told them I was her uncle."

Through a haze of tears, Jewel gave something that passed as a smile.

"I'm so sorry," she said. "I meant to ring you. I really did." The tears slipped from her eyes again and she attempted to wipe them away. "I can't seem to stop weeping." She shook her head as if to banish the moisture and then rubbed her eyes. "I don't know what's the matter with me!"

David smiled at her.

"You are just reacting to the accident with Jade. It's completely normal, you know."

"But ..."

"Sh," David interrupted. "Just let it happen. It's good for you. You've been putting on a brave face for so long you don't know what it is to be a little fragile."

Jewel pursed her lips, even as the tears still dribbled from her eyes. "I don't like this feeling," she moaned. "I don't like being weak and vulnerable, dependant on someone else. What if Jade doesn't get any better?" she fumbled in her handbag and found a tissue, dabbing at her eyes and looking at the smudges of mascara on the thin paper as if they were blood.

"Come on," David was quiet. "Drink up your coffee and I'll take you home. You can tell me all about it."

Jewel nodded and lifted the cup with a wobbly hand and drank. The steam from the liquid curled around her face giving the wet cheeks a shine and David was struck once more by the beauty of this woman, and his overwhelming desire to look after her. Maybe, now he could.

She put the cup down gently onto the table as if it would detonate on contact, looked up and smiled at David.

"Please, take me home. I'd like that." And together they rose. David took her to her car. Jewel had the presence of mind to look around for his vehicle. She tried to get into the driver's seat of her car. David stopped her with a hug. She looked at him.

"I'm fine," she said. "I'll drive – you need to get your car," but her eyes once more spilled tears. She wiped her face impatiently and David smiled.

Her words came out weak and uncertain. She still looked numb, and David merely ignored her comment as he steered her to the passenger side of her car.

"Don't worry about that," he said. "I'll come back later. I'll drive. You need to rest and I don't think you're really in any condition at the moment to get behind the wheel!"

He didn't wait for her to argue, and was amazed that she didn't even try. He moved around to the driver's side and was in the car and had started the engine before anymore was said. She couldn't even remember giving him the keys. She leaned back and closed her eyes. It was lovely to feel that she could trust David. She hadn't trusted any one for a long time.

David drove to his place and took Jewel up to the bed. The carpet was still stained, but he had got new crisp sheets on his bed. She made no comment as he undressed her and placed her gently down on the bed. He pulled up the covers and lay down on the top, fully dressed, beside her.

He cradled her in his arms, cuddling her for what seemed like hours. Finally he looked down and realised she was asleep.

He very, very carefully slid his arm from beneath her body, grimacing as the pins and needles attacked his arm. He slid off the bed, watching Jewel in case she awoke, but she continued to sleep.

He pulled up the covers again and tucked the blankets around her as if they were extensions of his own limbs.

It wasn't until he made it out into the lounge, having closed the door softly, leaving it open only a small crack in case she should need him, that he gritted his teeth and flexed his fingers until the feeling in his arm was almost normal. He made himself a sandwich and a cup of tea, and then he tiptoed to the door and sneaked a look into the bedroom.

Jewel was still in exactly the same position. The blankets were still tucked under her chin. She hadn't moved.

He watched her for a few minutes, wondering if she would be all right if she awoke while he went to get his car. She looked so vulnerable and he wanted so much to wrap her in his arms and make the sadness go away.

The sooner he left, the sooner he would be back to look after her. Jewel still slept on, so he decided to go.

He wrote a note explaining his decision, propped it up on the kitchen table and silently left his home.

***

When Topaz finally found the Moore Park Real Estate office, she wasn't happy. She stood and looked at the advertisements for houses that lined the windows. Then she re-read the note on the door.

This office is closed for the rest of the day due to family concerns. We're sorry for any inconvenience. We will be open tomorrow.

She shrugged. Well, it had been a long shot, and besides she really needed to get herself ready for tonight. She had another performance at 'The Blue Stocking' and Gus wouldn't understand if she didn't turn up. The worst part of it all was the fact that he would be expecting sex again tonight after the concert. Usually they were both high on adrenaline by then and it wasn't a problem, but tonight, Topaz knew she wouldn't be willing. Not only had Gus begun to annoy her, but also she wanted to get home and speak to Saffy, whatever the time was when she finished. She contemplated whether she should go to the police and write out a missing person's report.

Decision made, she went back to the car and drove to the local police station. By the time she had tried to explain to the police officer behind the desk that she didn't know how long Saffy had been missing, and that she was still expecting her to come home, she was over the whole justice system! The police officer showed no concern, telling her that her daughter was old enough to leave home, and perhaps she should come back in a week or two, if there still was no communication from her daughter. He looked at her as if it was her fault, that somehow she was a bad mother.

Topaz walked out of the station trying to control the anger inside. She realised that her vagueness and her ignorance of Saffy's whereabouts definitely made it look that way. Her inner turmoil was because she thought the police officer was probably correct!

What if Saffy was in danger? What if she had been abducted? Murdered? Lost?

So many scenarios crossed her mind – but the police hadn't been helpful at all. She felt like she could cry with frustration!

When Saffy finally arrived home, Saffy was going to talk to her – tell her she would change.

She drove home, unbidden tears rolling silently down her cheeks. She stopped in her garage and calmed herself, wiping the wetness from her face with the back of her hand. She got out of the car and slowly made her way inside her home.

She noticed the house was still silent, the bed in Saffy's room exactly as she had left it. Still Saffy wasn't home. Topaz checked the answering machine.

Nothing.

This was getting more and more worrying.

She decided to ring her mother. The phone answered after the first ring.

"Yes, Pearl here." The voice was loud and strident, and Topaz moved the phone away from her ear.

"Hi, Mum," she said. "Just ringing to find out if you'd heard from Saffy."

"No," Pearl answered. "Should I have?"

Topaz was forced to explain. Pearl listened without a word. When Topaz had finished speaking, there was a small hesitation on the line, then Pearl spoke

"I'll be right over."

"No...." but the phone was already dead.

Topaz looked at the handset as if it was still alive.

"Damn you, Mother," she declared to the inanimate machine. "I have to go out!"

***

The next day, Ruby awoke feeling terrible. She rolled over and groaned. Every bone in her body felt as if it was on fire.

A call of nature forced her to heave herself out of bed, and after visiting the bathroom, she went and made a cup of tea and some toast. Even this small task exhausted her. She took them back into her bedroom and went back to bed.

She sat there with an extra pillow behind her back while she ate and drank. She was astounded that a day out in town had pushed her to her limits. Her thoughts turned to the young girl lying in the hospital bed, but tiredness overcame her.

"Well, I'll just have to rest today. I'll go in and see Jade tomorrow".

With that thought, she carefully placed her plate and mug on the bedside table, snuggled down under the blankets and was asleep before she could count to ten.

***

Pearl decided to buy a ticket to Central Station. She could walk to Topaz's place from there, and it was so much easier than taking the car. There was nowhere safe to park around Topaz's place, any way. The last time she had taken the car, she'd parked it out in the street and some idiot had run in to it. It had cost her several hundred dollars to get the dents repaired. She wasn't going to have that happen again. Topaz was lucky she had a garage to house her car. Many of the homes in the area didn't have that luxury.

She hoped she would be there before dark. She didn't feel comfortable walking near the inner city after dark, and the way the days drew in quickly as winter approached, she hoped the trains were running on time and there were no hiccups on the way.

She bought the ticket with plenty of time to spare and waited at the platform.

While she waited she thought of Saffy.

When Topaz had told her she was pregnant, Pearl had been so disappointed with her daughter. Topaz had refused to tell her who the father was, and showed no interest in the baby when it finally arrived. But the little scrap had captivated Pearl. She been born with a shock of black hair and later her eyes had become a most entrancing green. Later the hair had decreased its intensity and settled for a light brown, but Pearl didn't care. She offered to look after her grand-daughter at every opportunity, and Topaz, with her busy schedule of socialising, rehearsals and performances had taken her up on the offers rapidly.

Now Saffy had grown into a pretty teenager. She had never really been a rebel during her earlier teen years, but what was happening now? Pearl was worried. When Saffy had gone through the traumas of watching her best friend die, then struggled with mental sickness, Pearl had felt so helpless. Something wasn't feeling right now. She hadn't heard anything at all from Saffy, and that wasn't normal.

Pearl got on the train and found a comfortable seat. It was lucky it wasn't peak hour – there were plenty of seats available and she could think without being annoyed. She stared out of the window and remembered her own past and all the dramas that had unfolded over the years.

It had all started in about 1950. She still remembered the cold of the streets in Berlin when she was only five. The German family that she had been with constantly reminded her that she was lucky. They told her they had taken her in at the end of the war out of the goodness of their hearts. She had been the child of a Jew, and before the war ended, a soldier had hoisted her on to them. They treated her with a certain amount of disdain, and punished her often for any small indiscretion she committed. When the chance had come for Pearl to escape, she had taken it. She was young, but determined.

Somehow she had escaped Germany and found herself hiding in a truck that took her to France. Eventually she had found a job, lying about her age, as she hadn't even been twelve at the time. She saved up furiously, living on the streets and scavenging food wherever she could.

When she had enough money, she bought a ticket on a cargo ship, which brought her to Australia. It was the only one that she could afford. Where the ship was going was none of her concern – as long as it was as far away from Germany as she could get.

The trip had been awful, with conditions bordering on diabolical. A small, unkempt bunk, in a small and dirty cabin with five other passengers. The food had been bland and monotonous, and because she hadn't spoken English very well, it had been lonely as well.

Once she had arrived in Melbourne in the late 1960's, she had married the first man who had shown her a little affection. It had been the worst decision of her life, because he had turned into a petty, thoroughly jealous man. That jealousy had caused him to question her every move, and when her answers weren't to his liking he had become violent.

Gradually the beatings eased, but that was generally because he was so drunk he couldn't stand up let alone punch or fight. One night he hadn't come home, and she had been relieved.

When there had been a knock on the door, she remembered opening it with reluctance, frightened that she would find him outside, without a key and not sufficiently drunk. It would have meant another night of torture if that had been the case. Instead, it had been the police.

"Excuse me," the policewoman said, and Pearl's heart leapt with fear. "Are you Mrs. Brown?"

Pearl had agreed slowly, but she was wary. Why did they want to know?

Then the policewoman spoke again, and the news hit Pearl hard.

Apparently her husband had become so drunk he had passed out in the middle of the road and been run over.

He was dead, and Pearl cried.

Not from grief, but from the release of tension, from the feeling of freedom and knowing she would never be afraid again. How she had managed to cope up until his death in 1986 she didn't like to think about. It was something she had thought was her punishment for leaving Germany.

Since then, she had tried to find out where she had really come from, and what had happened to her adoptive parents. Nothing was clear; so many documents had been lost during and just after the war. The only thing she had found out so far was that she had come from the jaws of a concentration camp, pulled from the Jewess's breast when she was beginning to toddle. The camp had been the notorious Auschwitz, and her mother…? That was the next thing she wanted to clarify.

She was pulled from her recollections by the disembodied voice that came out of the speaker above her head.

'The next station will be Central. The doors will automatically open when the train is stationery.'

Pearl grabbed her handbag and made her way to the doors, watching the platform and its' cargo of people as they came into view. The train stopped, and before she was engulfed in the herd of incoming passengers, she was on the platform, walking towards the main lobby.

***

When Saffy woke up, Rod was gone. She sat up and rubbed her eyes. The room was bathed in sunlight, but she had no idea what the time was.

It was necessary to find the bathroom, so she stretched, then stood. She vaguely remembered hearing the toilet flush, but she had been so nearly asleep, that she wasn't sure where it was. She hurriedly went through the door to the kitchen and looked around. There were two doors near the fridge so she went and opened them. It was a cupboard with a couple of items of food in it. She closed them and turned around slowly, looking at each wall. By now the call of nature was beginning to become urgent, and she hoped she could find the toilet before she ended up embarrassing herself. She had already had to go in the dark behind the baker's, but she had used the Station restrooms when it became necessary after that.

Footsteps coming up the stairs alerted her to the fact that either Rod was returning, or it was someone else. She didn't want to be caught here, but, as she looked around for somewhere to hide, she heard Rod come through the main door, whistling.

"You there, Saffy?" he called. "I got us some breakfast and the local paper."

Saffy popped her head around the kitchen door. "I'm here, but where's the toilet?" Rod smiled when he noticed that her legs appeared to be crossed.

He pointed.

"Didn't you remember I told you that it was up the front near the door?"

Saffy just clenched her teeth and dashed passed him, finding the door behind the partition that looked like mirrors.

Rod grinned. "I came back just in time, didn't I." Saffy heard him chuckling.

"Not funny!" she yelled through the closed door.

Rod was still smirking when she emerged and straightened her clothes. She scowled.

"Where'd you go?"

Rod pulled a sausage McMuffin out of a paper bag and handed it to her.

She devoured it in five seconds flat.

"Whoa! Steady on!" Rod exclaimed. "I only got you the one! Anyway, I got the 'Herald'. There seems to be no mention of an accident in the park occasioning death." He finished, flinging the paper down and suggesting she look at it.

Saffy let out a sigh. Had she told him about that last night? Or did she look like a murderer? Whatever that was supposed to look like!

Rod continued. "I think we'd better sit down and have a talk, now that you aren't quite so tired or wary."

Saffy nodded.

She glanced around at the space.

"Are you a ballet teacher?" she asked.

"No!" Rod laughed. "I told you that I was like you, and a friend helped me. Remember?"

Saffy nodded.

"Well, this is her ballet studio, but she has gone overseas for six months, and she asked me to look after the place while she was away, so it didn't get ransacked by vandals. It gave her peace of mind, and it's great for me – I won't have to find a place of my own for a while – and I don't have to pay rent for the time I'm here."

"Oh," Saffy didn't say any more.

"I know – lucky, eh? It's given me time to get some money behind me."

"How?"

"I've got a job, waiting on tables at a local caff, and they give me some food at the end of m' shifts, too!"

Saffy was suitably impressed.

"When do you work?" she asked.

"I'll have to leave you tonight, if you're still here. I've got a shift tonight. Before we go any further, we need to find out what you are going to do, tho'."

Saffy looked a little panicky.

Rod quickly reassured her. "You only have to tell me what you want to tell me," he said.

They sat in the beanbags and began to talk. Slowly Saffy relaxed. Then, without warning, it spilled out of her like tomato sauce out of a shaken bottle.

Rod sat quietly and listened. He made no comment, even when she went over what she had said last night, or when she repeated herself several times. He just let her talk. She cried often, her voice croaking with emotions at other times. She paced, she fidgeted and she ended sitting back down with a thump, looking at him beseechingly.

"And now I keep coming back to the same thing. I just don't know what to do!"

"I think the first thing you ought to try, is contacting your grandmother. She sounds as if she'd understand. Besides – you're still not sure if Jade is really dead. Perhaps she'll know." suggested Rod.

"She is, I'm sure of it! I saw her close her eyes, and everyone was so quiet, that I knew she had 'gone'."

Rod wasn't so sure. He looked at her quizzically.

"Mmmm. I still think you've got to check, and, if you think your mother won't help, or the police will be told, your grandmother sounds like your safest bet."

"I haven't got my phone." Saffy said quickly. "I left it home."

Rod didn't think that was much of an excuse. He handed her his.

"Ring her now."

Saffy shook her head doubtfully, hesitating to take the phone from his hand.

"Go on." He insisted. "Go on." He waved the phone in front of her.

She took it begrudgingly and pushed the buttons for Pearl's home. She listened, heart thumping. What would she say? Would her Oma already know the terrible thing she had done? Would she dob her in to the police? Would the police already be there?

She nearly cancelled the call, but the phone kept ringing.

No one answered.

She realised that Pearl was not at home. Now what was she going to do? Where was Pearl? It seemed like her run of luck lately. Just when she needed Oma she couldn't find her. She didn't know whether to be relieved, disappointed or worried.

10.

Topaz rang the hospital before she stepped into the shower. They still wouldn't tell her much, although they did inform her that there had been very little change, and that there had still been no teenage girl asking to visit. They reiterated that the 'family' limitation was still in force, and only an uncle had enquired.

The water from the shower eased the muscles in her back as she turned it towards the stream. She stood some time under the spray, trying to relax. Her mind was whirling! She had never known Saffy to stay away for so long.

Scenarios flashed through her mind, each more terrifying than the last. Was she lying somewhere, unconscious from her injuries? Was she injured? Nobody had told her anything! Maybe the incident that had put Jade in hospital, had left Saffy with amnesia – wandering around the streets not knowing who she was? Maybe she was dead? Or in her wanderings, been murdered by some street gang?

Where was she?

How was she going to sing tonight with all this worrying her? What was she going to do about Gus? Surely Saffy would be home by then? Maybe she could let Gus have one more 'quickie' in his office then tell him she wanted no more? No! She couldn't do that – he was paying her to perform at his club. She'd lose her job if she didn't do what he wanted. She HAD to keep her job so that Saffy could have as much as she can afford to give her.

I wonder where Saffy is?

Why has she disappeared?

Would Jade be OK?

Who the heck was Jade's Uncle?

Where do I start looking for Saffy?

When she stepped out of the shower and reached for the towel, Topaz hadn't actually cleaned herself. Her mind had slipped from one train of thought to another. She hadn't been able to focus. She turned back into the shower and grabbed the soap and shampoo.

She shook her head as if to clear the cobwebs. She spoke out aloud to the tiles as the water streamed onto her body.

"Get your act, together, Tope. Forget the job at the moment! You need to find Saffy, so calm yourself. Saffy is so much more important."

Then she soaped herself all over and washed her hair.

By the time she finally walked to her bedroom and got dressed she felt a lot calmer. The only thought that crossed her mind at the time was – *"When I see Saffy – boy – is she in trouble!"*

In the kitchen, she grabbed a piece of paper and pen, wrote Pearl a note, and, as she walked out, she attached it to the front door.

Hi Mum. Please ring me when you get here. I'll let you know where the spare key is. Go in and make yourself at home. I have a gig tonight. So I won't be home till about 3.00am. See you in the morning.

When she arrived at the club, she had put all the worries behind her and had on her professional face. She also knew, deep down, that she would be high enough with adrenaline after the performance to let Gus do what he wanted before she came home. She really didn't have any choice if she wanted to keep this job.

In fact, in some macabre sense, she was actually looking forward to the release, to the fetishism of some of Gus's sexual quirks – the 'punishments' he dealt out to her would be like an atonement for the results of her neglecting her daughter and the worry she was now experiencing. The bruises of his sexual obsessions would fade, but Topaz would always remember, and, instead of coping with the physical hurt as she normally did by letting herself enjoy the hurts at the time, she would ease it in her mind by thinking of Saffy. And Pearl – I wonder what she'll do? I hope she settles into the spare room and goes to sleep!

She just hoped she wouldn't be coming home to an empty house.

***

Jewel opened her eyes carefully. She recognised David's apartment, and wondered where he was. For a brief moment she couldn't remember why she was here and how she had got here, but then her brain seemed to explode with all the reasons.

She sat up and let the blankets slide off, putting her feet down onto the carpet. She was faintly aware of the aroma of stale wine oozing up between her toes and she looked down with distaste at the carpet. The red stains were still apparent from the debauched night not that long ago, and she closed her eyes again, trying to shut out the memory.

She stood, and padded her way into David's kitchen. There was no one there.

She looked around and noticed the note propped up on the table. It had been held in place by a mug in its front and a vase with a small flower, (she didn't know what, but thought it was a daisy of some sort) behind it.

She was still not dressed, but she wasn't cold, so she reached for the note and read it, as she turned to put the kettle on for a good strong cup of coffee. She definitely needed it. She remembered being so weak earlier and was ashamed of that weakness.

Had she really cried into his comforting chest?

Had she really mumbled and sobbed while he held her so warmly in his arms?

Had he held her while she slept, his body fully dressed whilst hers was naked?

What had he thought when it was revealed that she wore no underclothes?

Had she let her guard down and confessed more than she should have?

Her mind was still fuzzy and she couldn't recall exactly what she had said. However, she didn't think she had sought relief through sex, or that David had even suggested it.

She *did* remember that he had been understanding, loving and supportive. Somewhere within herself, she felt the first flush of guilt. She had never been so intimate with David, however uninhibited she acted when she was having sex with him. Last night she had finally dropped her barriers, surrendered to the emotions. That made her feel slightly alarmed, because even during raunchy and exhausting sex, she had always been able to control her feelings. She had still managed not to trust him or lower the façade. It made it much worse in her mind, because she knew that he loved her. Now, she stared at the little flower and knew it would be all right. That last night had taken their relationship to another level.

She picked up the note and read it again.

The note explained that he had gone to get his car, and that she was to stay there until he got back. He also said that he had closed the office for the day and not to worry. She was shocked. She realised that she hadn't thought about work since Doctor Rogers had spoken to her.

She poured the coffee into the mug she noticed on the kitchen table, then looked for the milk. She smiled to herself. David only had 'lite' milk in the fridge.

She sat, still unclothed, on the settee and held the mug in cupped hands, letting the heat filter into her body, her mind returning to the hospital. The image of her daughter, pale and gaunt, with her thumb in her mouth and her eyes blank, filled her mind. The flicker of recognition before she had slept was encouraging, but Jewel was still too stunned to work out what the future might hold.

She was still sitting there when David returned. He could see that she was thinking, and he guessed at the content of her thoughts. He tried to lighten the moment.

"Oh, Honey. You didn't have to greet me in that gorgeous gown."

Jewel turned slowly and looked at him, her eyes finally registering that he had walked in. She looked down at herself, placed her mug down on the coffee table, stood and dashed into the bedroom almost as if she was embarrassed by her nudity.

It occurred to David that he had never seen her so touchy about her naked form. As far as he was concerned it was a pleasure to behold at any time.

When she came out, she had slipped her dress on.

David opened his arms, and without a word she came to him.

He couldn't believe this was his hard and strong Jewel. He admitted to himself, though, that he had hoped for this transformation, although he would never tell this fact to Jewel.

He kissed the top of her head, and the curls tickled his nose. Suddenly it seemed so right to offer the comfort of his body, and he casually took off his shirt, then her dress.

She wasn't wearing anything underneath, and the feel of naked breasts on his bare chest was wonderful. Last night he had noticed that she had worn no underwear, but last night was about comfort in a different form.

Unlike their normal frantic need, this time there was no hurry, no urgency. They stood near the sofa just being together. David caressed her back; she ran her hands slowly over his chest. They kissed, long and tenderly. Jewel stifled a moan, and David felt himself become aroused. Neither of them moved.

When they stopped to breathe, David looked into her eyes. They were hooded with desire, and he asked.

"Would you like to go to the bedroom?" He waited, knowing that when she was in the grip of lust, anywhere would do. The coffee table, the kitchen bench or the tiles on the floor of the bathroom.

She looked up with a hesitancy and shyness that spoke of the new direction in their relationship.

"MM. Yes please." It was almost a whisper.

With hands clasped and lips once more together, they slowly made their way to the bed. David stopped to undo his trousers, dropping them and his underwear to the ground. Jewel stood by, looking at the length of his erection, and placing her hand gently on it. He inhaled sharply, but refused to succumb to the basic needs of his flesh. He lowered her lightly onto the bed, then, as she stretched her arms towards him, he went gladly into her arms. Finally he did what he had wanted to do for ages.

He loved her.

He found each silken piece of skin and kissed and honoured it. She began a tentative exploration of his body, but he stopped her.

"Just enjoy," he breathed against the skin.

He filled his senses with the scent of her. He nuzzled against the softness of her breasts. He got lost in the folds of her limbs and he once more drank from the wine of her lips. Slowly he moved along her body, until he tasted and worshiped at the core of her femininity.

Jewel melted under his caresses. She wanted so much to give him the same pleasure, and as his head sank between her legs, and he turned his body to lay over hers, she cradled his manhood, and pampered him in return.

Finally, with utmost care, he turned again, placed himself between her knees, lifted himself away from her body and looked at her. She looked deep into his eyes, and without a word, she opened herself to him and he entered her slowly and tenderly.

About an hour later, as they lay in each other's arms, snoozing and feeling wonderfully satisfied, the phone on the bedside table rang.

David reached over without moving Jewel and picked it up.

"Yes?" he said, somewhat dreamily.

"Yes," he answered a little more briskly this time. He handed the phone to Jewel.

"It's the hospital."

Jewel opened her eyes and was properly awake within moments.

"I'm here," she said into the phone. There was silence for a short while as she listened.

"I'll be there as soon as I can."

She passed the phone back to David and he put it down.

"She's asking for me," she said, already half out of bed and moving towards the shower.

"Will you come with me?" she added, and David gladly agreed.

They were on the road before the sun had finished sliding into the next hemisphere.

***

Pearl arrived at Topaz's house and read the note. How on earth her daughter expected her to ring when she didn't own a mobile phone, Pearl didn't know. She didn't want one of those new-fangled things. If people couldn't catch her – then too bad. They would have to wait until she was home. The new 'mobiles', as they were called, probably wouldn't last much longer – it was only a fad for the younger generation as far as she was concerned.

She backtracked along the road to a public phone-box she had noticed on her way from the station. They seemed to be harder and harder to find these days. She took her address book out of her handbag and looked for the number. When she stepped into the box, she wrinkled her nose. It smelled strongly of cat, and the graffiti on the walls suggested *'if you want a head-job, call Samantha'* and there were several suggestive drawings and rude words scrawled around the comment.

The phone was barely working, and even though she couldn't hear very well, Pearl didn't want to hold it too close to her ear, as it was dirty and partly broken.

She yelled into the phone when Topaz finally answered.

"Where's the key?"

Topaz held her phone away from her ear, too. The reason, however, wasn't the same. It was expedient when her mother was on the phone, otherwise she was sure she would get a damaged ear-drum.

"For goodness sake, Mum," Topaz yelled in her turn. "Tone it down, will ya'. You're not talking to me on the other side of the world without the benefit of a phone."

"Sorry, love." Pearl said.

It made no difference. Her voice still quite brassy, she asked for the key again.

When she had the information, she hung up and started back to Topaz's place, pleased to leave the smelly, claustrophobic box.

She got there and let herself in. A cup of tea was her next stop, and she sat and tried to think what she would do until Topaz came home.

Where would she start looking for Saffy?

Why was Saffy not here?

Why didn't Topaz do more searching?

What, in fact, was going on?

She sat at the kitchen bench, the cup of tea steaming up her glasses, and thought back over her life again, wondering whether she could have done anything different.

When her husband had died it had been difficult to keep everything balanced. She had to find a job to pay the bills. She had still been shy of people – the fear that her husband would beat her if she looked at anyone else was so entrenched that it had taken a lot of courage to squash it. Working in the factory sorting small parts for engines was boring, and she had had to do long hours to get the money she needed.

Bills that she thought had been paid started to come in, and she discovered she was in debt to the electric company, the local supermarket and the phone service. Her husband had been using their money to buy alcohol and, for all she knew, drugs as well. She had felt horrified that she hadn't known. That he had kept her so frightened that she hadn't wanted to know.

Topaz had been at an awkward age, just entering into the teenage years, and Pearl thought she had probably let her down. She hadn't been there to support and encourage her. She had been working too hard at the time. Too hard at trying to find the strong person she had been before her marriage. When Topaz had fallen pregnant, Life had once more become complicated.

Pearl blamed herself.

After the baby was born, Topaz hurled herself into her singing. Pearl watched as a succession of one boyfriend after another trailed after Topaz. Somewhere along the way the baby, Sapphire, had slipped from Topaz's priorities.

Pearl remembered the time well.

As Topaz's career began to take off, Saffy's welfare was almost left to the fates of congenial neighbours and patrons of every pub and club that Topaz sang at.

How many men friends Topaz had was beyond Pearl's understanding. She never settled down and, Pearl thought, now she never would.

Pearl had been working so many hours then, that she had not been able to look after either Topaz or her grand-daughter. She recalled watching as Topaz became more and more out of control, and Saffy had slipped from childhood into her teen years with insecurities so big she had found it difficult to relate to anyone.

The tea grew cold, and Pearl made another. She searched through the cupboards until she found something to eat and settled herself down in front of the television. She decided to wait until Topaz came home.

A reality show was on, and Pearl surfed through the few channels available. Nothing caught her interest, so she left the reality program going. Eventually, she fell asleep, curled up on the sofa, with a blanket over her.

***

Saffy tried to contact Oma several times during the morning. It was useless. No one answered and Pearl didn't have an answering machine, so she couldn't leave a message. Not that she would have. The police were probably waiting for her so they could work out where she was and come and get her.

Rod tried to get her to ring her mother.

"Surely your Mum will be worried?" he remarked. "At least let her know you're all right."

Saffy refused and kept refusing every time Rod mentioned it.

They ate some baked beans on toast for lunch, then Rod suggested they get out and go for a walk.

Saffy didn't want to. She was sure that she was a 'wanted woman' and that police would be everywhere. Rod tried to convince her that that wasn't the case.

He ventured outside, then came back about ten minutes later with a newspaper and a coke.

He put the paper on the floor, and Saffy poured over every page.

"I told you," Rod confirmed again and again. "There were no police outside when I looked. In fact I saw none at all when I walked to the newsagency and got the paper. And there is nothing in the paper about a girl dying at the local park. I told you that before."

Saffy could not be convinced.

"I'm not going out there." Saffy declared.

"Well, OK." Rod knew from previous experience that forcing the issue wasn't going to help.

"I just ask you to think about it," he said

"Where are you going?" Saffy furrowed her brow and looked confused when Rod turned away and seemed to ignore her.

"I told you before," Rod said calmly. "I have to go to work shortly. I will be gone until about midnight."

Saffy nodded.

"Yes, I know," she agreed as if she hadn't been puzzled moments before.

"Well, while I'm away, think about ringing your mother. She has an answering service, surely."

When Saffy nodded, he continued before she could refuse again. "At least let her know you are safe."

Saffy shrugged. "Maybe."

Rod thought that sounded at least like a bit of progress so he didn't pursue it further.

They sat in the beanbags for a while, relaxing. They talked about their favourite pop stars, films and books.

"There's some books and magazines in the kitchen cupboard, or you can watch a bit of telly," Rod suggested. "The telly is really small, and the reception isn't much chop – a bit snowy – but you can watch it if you want." then Rod got ready and went off to work.

Saffy found a book in the cupboard and settled down to read for the evening.

***

When Rod had gone, the studio felt strange and eerie. There were creaks and groans that set Saffy's teeth on edge. The traffic outside sent shadows flitting across the back wall and the sounds of footsteps on the street outside echoed up the stairwell until she thought there were crowds of people coming to get her. In amongst all the sound, she couldn't stand the silence.

She turned the TV on, just so there were voices and music that drowned out the loneliness and the fears. The program didn't help. It was a re-run of *'Nightmare on Elm Street'* and she turned it to another channel. Re-runs of *'Gilligan's Island'* were a little better.

As she squinted at the screen, her mind bubbled over with the scene at the park. She should never have shouted at Brad. That was Jade's horse's last straw. The car backfire had frightened the horse, but the shout at caused the horse to buck Jade off. Would she ever be able to get the image of Jade lying crumpled on the ground? The TV kept blaring, but nothing could stop her feelings of dread, her fear of being discovered and her sudden awareness of her helplessness.

She got up and walked around, trying to ease her growing terror. When she felt a little better she went into the kitchen and searched the cupboards for some munchies. She found a packet of potato chips and some cigarettes in a packet hidden under the towels. After further searching she found some matches.

This would have to do.

She went back to the beanbags, sat down and glared through the snow at the TV. The snow made it almost impossible to see a picture, but the sound was comforting. She opened the chips and began to eat.

With shaking fingers she lit a cigarette. She had never smoked before, and the acrid smoke made her cough. After several more puffs, her head felt a little fuzzy and she felt sick. She persevered, sucking some more into her lungs, but she stubbed it out in the saucer she was using as an ashtray, and raced over to the toilet where she vomited into the bowl. The floor felt cold and unforgiving, and her head whirled. She couldn't seem to focus her eyes, and when she stood, she thought she would be sick again.

She staggered over to the beanbags and collapsed.

Just after nine o'clock, Rod came running up the steps and found her slumped on the floor. Her head was on the beanbag, but her body hadn't made it.

She looked up at him, bleary-eyed.

"Whatya' doing home?"

Rod shook his head in disbelief. She looked terrible.

"I'm on a break. Thought I'd check to see if you're OK."

Saffy tried to sit up. She wasn't going anywhere. She sunk back onto the beanbag. Rod's face changed. She had never seen him so angry.

"Fuck!" Rod exploded. "You've been through the cupboards, haven't you? Did you find the joints I'd stashed?"

Saffy giggled.

"You're stoned," he said, shaking her by the shoulders. "Damn! When you've come back to earth, think about what you should do – ring your mother!" With that he stormed back out of the studio and after the door slammed, sending vibrations right through the floor and all of her bones, Saffy heard him run down the stairs and out into the street.

She wanted to stop him. To run after him and say she was sorry, but she couldn't have got up if her life had depended on it. She sank back down and, as the world whirled, she went to sleep.

***

When she woke up, she felt a lot better. The large clock on the wall showed her it was about eleven thirty. As it was dark, and Rod still wasn't home, it was obviously the same night.

Saffy sat still for a few minutes having a debate inside her head. Should she call her mother? What would she say? Hang on a minute, her mother would still be at the club! If she rang, she could talk into the answering machine, and there would be no one to ask questions. Why hadn't she thought of that before? It was the perfect solution!

Before she could change her mind, she sat up, waited for the dizziness to settle and then stood ready to ring her mother. She felt in her pockets for her mobile. *"That's right – she'd left it on her bed at home – it had run out of charge."*

Then she realised that Rod had his phone with him, so she would have to either wait for him to return, or go and find a public phone box. That thought didn't sound very pleasant. She didn't want to go outside. On the other hand, now that she had decided to ring, she wanted it done, without Rod breathing down her neck. She only had to let her mum know that she was safe. It would only take a few minutes.

She bundled herself into one of Rod's hoodies that was on the floor near her, and went.

11.

When Jewel and David got to the hospital it was dark.

Jewel was nervous, and David tried to calm her down.

"We don't know exactly how Jade is," he commented as they walked into the lift to take them up to Jade's room. "but being uptight and jittery isn't going to help Jade."

Jewel nodded.

"I know," she sighed. "I just can't help it. What if she is worse? What if she doesn't recognise me?"

David smiled. "Honey! She asked for you. In my mind that means there has been an improvement."

Jewel took a deep breath, breathing out several times to calm herself. David put his arm around her.

"Come on, love, put a smile on the dial! We'll face this together. I'm here for you and Jade."

Jewel looked at him with gratitude.

"Thanks, David. After all I've done, I feel bad asking you to take on this burden."

David was amazed that Jewel was saying these words to him, but he didn't show it on his face.

"It's OK! I want to help."

Jewel gave him a flicker of a smile. Then she visibly pulled herself together, lifted her chin and straightened up. Together, holding hands, they walked up to Ward seven, and into room fifteen.

***

Jade was sitting up in bed. A plate with a half-eaten sandwich as well as a nearly empty glass of orange juice was on the tray next to her.

She smiled as Jewel walked into the room.

"Hello, Mummy," she said, albeit a little uncertainly. She looked at David with a frown. She didn't seem to know who he was.

The head nurse came into the room and asked David to come with her, leaving Jewel alone with her daughter.

"Excuse me, sir," she said quietly. "Can I have a word?"

David looked over at Jewel. She was kissing Jade on the forehead and holding Jade's hand and smiling. Jade looked up into her mother's face and a light of recognition shone out of her eyes.

David followed the head nurse. He felt satisfied that they would be all right.

The head nurse took him a little way along the corridor and stopped. She faced him and smiled.

"I presume you are Jade's father?"

David didn't know whether he should agree or not. Immediately he shook away the lie, and told the nurse he was Jewel's partner, not Jade's father.

"Oh! OK!" The head nurse didn't question his terminology. David wasn't quite sure if he had said the right thing, but then, when the nurse continued, he knew he had.

"Well, sir. Will you be able stand by Jade's mother during this time?"

David didn't hesitate.

"Of course." His answer was definite. "I have already told her we will face this together. Is there anything you need to tell me?"

The head nurse was adamant. "I would like to tell you both together, "she said, "but I needed to ascertain your relationship first, and to allow time for Jade and her mother to bond again."

David nodded.

Before the nurse could leave, David asked.

"Listen, I just want to know if I can tell Jade's mother good news or bad news. I would like to be able to support her, whatever the answer is. You don't have to give me specifics – that can wait till we are together. Just tell me – good or bad?"

The nurse thought for a moment.

"We…ll," she hesitated. "I'd still prefer to talk to you together – but just at the moment, let's say – we are cautiously optimistic."

David nodded again.

"Good. Now, is it OK if I go back and see how Jade and Jewel are getting along?"

The nurse was the one who nodded this time. David said goodbye and strode back to Jade's room

***

Ruby slept most of the day. About three o'clock she woke and pushed Punch off the bed. He yowled with displeasure.

"You naughty cat," Ruby complained. "My legs are numb from your weight on them! You know you're not allowed on the bed!"

She struggled into her slippers and wrapped her dressing gown around her shoulders. She picked up the cup and plate off of the bedside table and shuffled into the kitchen.

When she realised she had slept the day away she was most upset.

"I'll have a cuppa, then watch some TV. Darn! I guess I'll have to check on Jade tomorrow," she told Punch as he rubbed his body on her legs and meowed at her for some food.

Placing the mug on a tray, she managed to find a couple of biscuits in the fridge for afternoon tea. She opened a tin of cat-food and placed some in Punch's dish beside the fridge. While Punch was occupied with his dinner, she took the tray into the lounge and turned on the TV, sinking back into her comfy armchair. The biscuits tasted like sawdust, but the tea was refreshing. She drank it almost in one swallow.

Ruby sat and watched another re-run of *'Gilligan's Island'*, until the screen became a blur and she slept once more.

It was midnight before she awoke again.

***

Once Saffy was outside, her courage deserted her. The street was in darkness. Someone had broken the street light on the corner, and there seemed to be shadows moving wherever she looked. She had forgotten how eerie the streets at night could be.

The worst thing of all, was that now she knew that even while most people were safe and asleep in their beds, there was still activities happening that were only possible during the dark hours. The memory of what she had witnessed only a couple of short days ago were still vivid in her mind.

She hesitated.

Should she go back to Rod's place? Should she forget finding a public phone box? Should she wait for Rod to return from work? She looked around again, flinched inside at the possibilities behind each obstacle, each dark area made her brain wriggle with fingers of fright. She swallowed, licked her lips, then, with clenched teeth, decided, now that she was out here, it was silly to give up.

Travelling on adrenaline, she dashed down the road, turned the corner, saw the phone box and, before she could change her mind dropped the few coins into the slot and dialled her mother's number.

The answering service's voice requested the caller to leave a message!

Saffy breathed again. Mum was out – she didn't need to face any questions.

She waited for the beep, then spoke in to the machine.

"Hi Mum, Just thought you'd like to know, I'm staying with a friend. I'm safe. Bye"

She slammed down the receiver and ran all the way back to Rod's studio.

Once she was inside, she leaned on the door and waited until her breathing got back to normal and her heart had stopped thumping. Then she walked over to the beanbag and sank into it, pulling the blanket over her. She stayed that way for a long time, eyes open and staring at the ceiling.

At Topaz's home, Pearl awoke with a start from the sofa, suddenly aware that the answering service had clicked in and she could hear Saffy's voice. By the time she dragged herself up and lunged for the phone, Saffy was gone.

***

At 'The Blue Stocking', Topaz finished the last round of songs. The clients were all drunk now and the whole place was jumping. The level of noise was so high that any more singing she could have done would have been lost. The in house recorded music took over.

She went over to the bar.

"Give me a Whisky on the rocks, will you, Jim."

Jim looked at her with one raised eyebrow.

"Not feeling too happy, eh?" he asked. "You look really down!"

"Yeah – well – things aren't going too well at home at the moment," Topaz took the glass from Jim's hand as she spoke.

Jim waited for a moment for Topaz to explain, but she said no more, merely drained the glass and handed it back.

"Top it up again, there's a dear," she said and Jim did.

With the glass still in her hand, Topaz walked up to Gus's office and knocked on his door. She wasn't looking forward to telling him it was all over.

She didn't wait for Gus to say anything. She opened the door and walked in.

Gus was holding one of the bar girls down over the desk, her face buried in the papers, her skirt hitched up over her back, her knickers on the floor, and he was up to the hilt in her. His fingers were up her anus at the same time. His face was contorted in ecstasy, but the girl was trying desperately to hold on to the desk, legs splayed like a giraffe drinking. Topaz knew exactly how she felt. She had been in that position more than once, with her buttocks so far apart that she felt like her body would be ripped in half. She couldn't see the girl's face, but she imagined she would be grimacing in pain.

Gus almost snarled a smile. He was obviously close to coming, but he pulled out and grinned.

"Come and join us," he said his dick still quivering, upright and glistening with the girl's lubrication, his hand still pushing an extra finger into her rectum. The girl on the desk lay exposed and breathing with some relief coupled with a groan of agony as Gus added his thumb, looked down with a grin and stabbed into her with some force.

Topaz didn't wait to see what he would do next. The girl was not enjoying the punishment, although Gus obviously was. She just shook her head in disgust, turned and walked out of the office and out of the club. She wouldn't be singing there again.

***

Pearl greeted her at the door.

"I heard the car," Pearl looked excited.

Topaz strode passed her and threw her handbag on the sofa.

"What are you still doing up?" she said tiredly to Pearl.

"I actually fell asleep on the sofa," Pearl admitted. "But, guess what?"

Topaz sighed and shook her head, Pearl's harsh voice reverberating in her head like an imprisoned wasp.

"God, Mum! I'm not in the mood to play games. I'm tired and I've had a lousy night."

"Well, this should make you feel better," Pearl was almost gloating. "There's a message from Saffy on the answering machine."

"What?" Topaz strode over to the telephone table and clicked on the message.

When the short message was over, she glared at her mother.

"Well, that's not much help!" she snapped. "Why didn't you talk to her and find out where she was?"

Pearl had the decency to look ashamed.

"Um, sorry!" she said. "I was actually asleep when the call came in, and by the time I got up and lifted the phone, she was gone!"

"Damn! Damn! Damn," Topaz swung around and headed to the kitchen to pour herself a glass of wine.

Pearl followed her. "That's not going to help!" she scolded.

Topaz turned and lifted her hands in frustration.

"Shit! Mum. I'm not a teenager anymore – you don't have to tell me what to do!" Topaz pulled the cork and poured a large glassful. "And now, not only don't I know where Saffy is, I don't have a job either!" and she tipped the glass and swallowed half its' contents in one gulp!

"What?" Pearl was bewildered. "Why? When did that happen?"

Topaz threw her hands up in the air.

"You have no idea what goes on at the club. And what with Saffy disappearing and Jade's accident – I've had enough! I walked out!"

"Perhaps you should go back, rethink the decision. You need the money!" Pearl's strident voice was getting on Topaz's nerves.

"No way!" she declared, after emptying the glass in her hand again. She emptied the rest of the bottle into the glass and moved the bottle to the sink.

"Look, Mum, I'm sorry. I'm too tired to discuss this with you at the moment. I'm going to bed."

Pearl was left standing in the kitchen as Topaz disappeared into her room.

***

David walked back into Jade's room in time to see Jewel kiss Jade on the forehead. Jade had a small smile on her face, and her eyes closed.

Jewel turned to David.

"She seems to be about 10 years old now. That's better than she was. She knew who I was, and who she was!"

"That's great," David said quietly. "Perhaps that's a good sign!"

Jewel let out a breath with a rush.

"Gosh I hope so!"

"Is she asleep?"

Jewel looked at Jade, and caressed her hand.

"Mmm. I think so."

"In that case, you should be able to leave her for the moment. The head nurse wants a word."

Immediately a look of panic flickered across Jewel's face.

"Oh?"

"It's OK," David smiled. "She just wants to update you on Jade's condition."

Jewel let Jade's hand slip softly from under her fingers and stood up. With a last look at Jade, she followed David out of the room, and they made their way to the nurses' station.

The head nurse was sitting at the computer, but she immediately stood and came over to them. She smiled.

"If you would like to follow me, we'll go into the consulting room along here and be a little more comfortable while we chat. Would you like a cup of coffee or tea?"

David looked at Jewel and raised one eyebrow questioningly.

"No thanks," Jewel answered. She was too nervous to drink or eat.

The nurse moved out from behind the desk and Jewel and David walked behind her to the room, where they were offered some comfortable chairs to sit in. Jewel perched on the edge of hers and looked expectantly at the nurse. She was nervous, anticipating the worst scenario.

The nurse could feel the tension.

"Mrs. Sutcliffe. Please relax. I only have good news for you!"

David saw the stiffness leave Jewel's shoulders and she began to breathe more normally.

"Oh, that's wonderful!"

"Before you get too excited, though, you must understand that there is still a long way to go." The nurse looked from one to the other in front of her.

Jewel nodded and David reached for her hand.

"You've already spoken to her doctor?"

Jewel nodded again.

"Good. He asked me to tell you that all the signs are positive."

Before either David or Jewel could interrupt, she went on.

"The swelling on her brain seems to be going down at a normal rate, and the bruising that had been causing the anomaly in her age is also decreasing. She seems to be gaining her memory slowly, so we are optimistic that she will continue to improve."

Jewel looked ecstatic with the news.

The nurse continued. "In another few days, if her recovery continues as it is at the moment, I think we will be able to discharge her from the hospital."

"That's such good news," David remarked.

"Yes, I guess it is." The nurse smiled at him. "You must realise though that she is still very fragile. We will be monitoring her for some time as an outpatient, and any deterioration in her condition will see her re-admitted to the hospital immediately.

"Can we go and sit with her for a while?" Jewel asked.

"Yes, of course. However, it is late, so not too long please."

Jewel and David arose and they filed out of the room.

"Thank you," Jewel said as they parted at the nurses' station and the head nurse went back to her computer readout. David concurred, murmuring his thanks as well.

They sat quietly next to Jade's bed for another hour. When she didn't stir, David gently suggested that they go home. He was still struggling with the complete change in Jewel.

Jewel was reluctant, but she followed David out of the hospital into the dark of the night. Their car looked lonely in the car park. They got in and drove away.

***

Ruby looked at the clock and sighed. She wanted to go back to sleep, but her body couldn't relax again. The TV was still hissing at her, so she needed to turn it off. Her thoughts centred on the accident and once again she wondered how both Jade and Saffy were coping. Then she began to think of the ramifications for each girl's family. She knew nothing about their families, and the more she thought the more she wanted to find out. She definitely needed to go and visit Jade in the morning.

Eventually she groaned and pushed herself out of the armchair, her leg muscles still sore from the lack of movement. Every bone and muscle in her body hurt. She creaked to an almost upright position as she slipped her feet into her dirty pink slippers. Ruby didn't think it was still reaction to her dash a couple of days ago. She felt every moment of her 77 years. There was no point in getting into bed then tossing and turning, so, after she turned off the telly, she dragged herself out to the kitchen and put the kettle on.

Punch meowed loudly and prowled around her until she gave in and let him out. He disappeared into the night, and before the kettle boiled he was back scratching at the door.

Ruby let him in and padded to the kettle, filling up her mug with steaming water, using the extra water to fill her hot water bottle. She took the tea into the bedroom and got into bed, cuddling the hot water bottle. She picked up the book she was reading off of the bedside table and settled down to a good read.

No sooner had she drunk the tea than she lost all her energy, and she snuggled down. Punch cuddled down next to her, and two different levels of gentle snores indicated that they were both asleep again.

12.

The next day dawned overcast and dreary. Ruby turned over in bed and hauled the blanket up around her shoulders. Punch shifted a little to find the warmth in the bed behind Ruby's back.

Topaz moaned, looked at the clock and decided to sleep for another hour.

Pearl got up and made some porridge and then sat at the kitchen table wrapped in the dressing gown she had discovered in the hall cupboard. She found a crossword book in the bookshelf and started doing the first one she found that Topaz hadn't started.

Jewel merely cuddled further into David's arms.

Jade awoke and wondered where she was. Her memory was a little hazy, but she vaguely remembered being in the park on her horse.

Saffy awoke still curled up in the beanbag. She hadn't heard Rod come in, but he had placed another blanket over her.

She looked around. She must have made a sound, because Rod poked his head around the kitchen door and grinned. A pleasant smell issued from the depths.

"Wakey, wakey," he trilled. Saffy looked at him with daggers spearing from her half-open eyes.

He wasn't a bit perturbed.

"Bacon and eggs almost ready. Up you get!"

Saffy relaxed. What she wouldn't do for a plate of bacon and eggs. She stood up and finger-combed her hair. The curls were only half tamed by the action.

While they sat companionably eating breakfast, Rod spoke.

"Did you ring your Mum?" He didn't look at Saffy, but kept his eyes on his plate. The reaction from her was just as he expected.

"What do you think?" she said sarcastically. "I had no mobile – mine's on my bed at home, and you had yours!"

Rod shrugged.

"Eh! Sorry! You can use mine now, if you want."

"Too bloody late," Saffy answered somewhat sulkily. "I ended up going to the local phone box up the street, and left a message that I was safe. Is that OK with you?" She had put down her fork, put her hand on her hip and spat the last sentence.

"Whoa – OK!" Rod widened his eyes and shook his hands in front of him as if he could push her away. "I wasn't trying to be a nuisance – only trying to help!"

Saffy relaxed and went back to her food.

"Yeah! I know," she mumbled. "I don't mean to jump down your throat. I know you're only trying to help."

Rod didn't say a word.

Saffy looked up at him.

"You've done nothing but help. Sorry! But, you know, I'm feeling a bit fragile this morning – AND I was a little paranoid last night when I had to go outside!"

"Yep! That would be the fault of getting stoned on the joints you found in the drawer last night." Rod suddenly grinned. "I was going to get rid of those later – or sell them to a friend! – It's one way of making a little pocket money on the side." He wiggled his eyebrows up and down a la Groucho Marx. He did the actions of holding a cigar in his fingers.

"Isn't it illegal?" Saffy asked.

"Of course," Rod laughed.

Suddenly Saffy was worried. The police could come for Rod, and then she'd be caught, too! She decided that she had to leave as soon as possible. As soon as Rod went out, she'd make a run for it.

Rod saw a look of panic come over Saffy, and he decided to drop the subject. Considering he didn't touch drugs, and he'd had to hide the joints his friend had left with him, Rod thought the whole situation was rather amusing. He had no idea just how distraught Saffy was.

***

When Topaz came out of her bedroom, she hadn't even done her hair. She put her hand on Pearl's shoulders.

"Eh, Mum. Sorry about last night."

"That's OK. I should have spoken to Saffy when she rang – I didn't think she'd go so quickly." Pearl looked up from her crossword. "Gawd! You look terrible. You OK?"

Topaz smiled.

"It's been a long time since you've seen me first thing in the morning," she puckered up her nose. "I never put even a little toe outside until I've 'done' my face!"

Pearl nodded. "Yeah! I understand. I try to keep my hair dyed all the time, too! It wouldn't do to admit I'm going grey!"

Mother and daughter looked at one another, both finding it funny that they didn't normally tell each other their little secrets. It was ground breaking!

"You know, Mum." Topaz pulled out the chair next to her mother and sat down. She put her elbows on the table and cradled her chin in her hands. "We should do this more often."

Pearl agreed.

"We were never very good at communicating, were we?" she said.

Topaz shook her head. "No – I guess not. There are an awful lot of things I never told you about my life!"

Pearl raised her head and stretched.

"Same here!" she commented. "Saffy's disappearance and Jade's accident just goes to show you how we take life so much for granted. We should take every moment that we have and make it the best that we can!"

"True!" Topaz nodded, then stood.

"After coffee, I'm going in to see Jade. You coming?"

"Absolutely. After that, if Jade can't give us the information about Saffy, we have to start looking for her." Pearl got up and walked to the phone. She turned and spoke to Topaz.

"I'll just ring the hospital and see if they've relaxed the 'family only' rule".

"Good idea," Topaz filled her mug with boiling water and brought it back to the table.

She sat and gazed into nothing. The images that sprang into mind were all the things in the past that she had never told her mother, and she was still undecided whether she ever would.

***

She gazed up to the ceiling from her bed and tried to sleep. But sleep wouldn't come.

She was so excited. Tomorrow was her tenth birthday. She'd made it to double figures! She wondered what present she would get. She already knew, at her age, that money was tight. Her mother had trouble putting food on the table, let alone putting money away for a gift. Her Dad always used the money on grog; it made her Mum really cranky.

Topaz knew to keep out of his way when he got home. When he was drunk, he was also violent. Mum often bore the brunt of his anger, having to stay hidden for days until the bruising faded. Topaz knew to hide as soon as she heard him at the door. Thank goodness she could disappear into her own room at such times.

Tonight had been different. She had retreated to her room early. At least there was the excitement and the anticipation of tomorrow and her birthday.

Topaz heard her father arrive home. Almost immediately the shouting and thumping began. She pulled the pillow over her head and tried to stop the sound. The excitement about her birthday tomorrow had been destroyed as she heard her mother's whimpers, and her father's swearing. Curled up in a little ball, she tried and tried to will it to stop.

When it did, she was surprised.

The door of her bedroom opened and she sat up quickly.

"Mum…" but her voice faltered.

Her father swayed into the room. There was a stupid grin on his face.

"Honey? You awake?" he slurred. "Yer Mum couldn't shtay awake after I shwiped her one for waitin' up for me! I got her to fall on the floor. It looked sho pretty that I had to kick her when she didn't move!"

Topaz held her breath as he staggered towards her.

The indignity of the actions that he took after that were horrifying. He had stepped out of his trousers and shown her his private parts. Then he tore off her nightie and used her as if she was his wife.

He visited her almost every night after that, once Pearl had gone to sleep. It became a hated ritual that Topaz had no way of escaping. She was so embarrassed, but knew not to say a word. She wondered what she had done wrong to cause her father to do this to her, specially when he smiled afterwards and told her not to tell anyone, that it was their very special secret. She knew her father would belt her within an inch of her life if she even whispered one word to anyone. And she knew her mother would also get more beatings.

Since she had become a vessel for his lust, the number of assaults on Pearl had diminished considerably. Topaz didn't want her to be beaten again, so she gritted her teeth and allowed her father the liberties he took.

The night the police had come to the door to inform them of his death had been a relief, the relief of freedom from his advances. Topaz hadn't been sorry to see him go. She had no concept that her mother felt the same way.

It was about three months later that she had discovered she was pregnant. There was no way she would tell her mother that the baby was her own father's. The only way out of the dilemma was to suddenly become a social butterfly.

For some time she couldn't even look at the baby. Had no feelings for the outcome of her father's lust. She went out with as many boys and men as she could, keeping them all at arms length, frightened of the intimacy that she had been forced to endure at such a young age. That was when she discovered that she could sing at pubs and clubs, at the same time and drinking to dull the memories.

She became the local 'bike' as far as her mother was concerned. Pearl thought it was reaction to the loss of her father, although if she had asked even one of the males she brought home, she would have discovered there was no sex involved at all. Topaz only began to be sexually active after Saffy was about five and at school. By then she didn't care anymore. Sex was just a sideline – after all that's what all the men wanted, just like her father. She already felt soiled, so her body was for the pleasure only of men. She was tough and free with her favours.

What did it matter. It gave her the means to achieve success in the entertainment game. She gave them what they demanded, and then moved on to someone else.

***

"Finished your coffee?" Pearl asked.

Topaz came out of her trance.

"Eh?"

"The hospital has said we can go in and visit Jade. That must mean she's getting better. Hurry up and get ready!"

Topaz rubbed her eyes, swallowed the last dregs of her coffee, and disappeared into the bedroom to get dressed. She was looking forward to asking Jade what had happened. Perhaps she would be able to find out about the friend that Saffy was staying with. She still couldn't understand why she hadn't come home.

"Won't be long," she said over her shoulder. "Hope you'll be ready when I come out! You've got ten minutes!"

***

David kissed Jewel on the top of her head. She smelled good. Last night had been a glorious celebration of the new Jewel. No obsessions, no kinky behaviour and no insatiability. David was in seventh heaven. Jewel had finally found feelings. Now he realised that had been the missing ingredient before.

He bent towards her and whispered gently into her ear.

"Wake up, Honey."

"Mmmm?" Jewel snuggled into his arms a little more and David squeezed her a little, smiling as he did so.

"Come on, love. It's time to get up so that we can go and see Jade."

Jewel's eyes opened and she pushed herself away from him.

"Oh my gosh!" she breathed, and David felt bereft as she turned and got out of bed. He revelled in watching her nakedness as she walked into the bathroom.

He heaved a sigh as he also rolled over and stood up. The closeness that they had experienced since Jewel had spoken to Jade's doctor was something he didn't want to lose. It was still like a miracle to him. He had wanted this for so long, and he felt guilty that he had got it only by way of the accident. He just hoped it would continue.

At David's insistence they sat and had breakfast. Jewel fidgeted the whole time until they were ready to leave.

The drive to the hospital was slow and steady. The rain made for treacherous conditions, and several times David had to brake suddenly. Jewel was silent and tense throughout the journey.

When they walked into Jade's room, Jade was smiling. Jewel relaxed.

***

Ruby groaned as she forced her body to get out of bed. Punch was already prowling around the back door, yowling loudly. Ruby let him out, looked out into the dismal day, shivered, then went back and got her dressing gown. It was cold. There was no money for the heater, so she boiled the kettle and filled her hot water bottle again.

After Punch came in, she placed a bowl of warm milk down with his breakfast, then took her cup of tea into the lounge. On the way she flicked on the radio and Weber's clarinet concerto washed over her. She covered her legs with a crocheted rug, tucked the hot water bottle behind her back and sat with her eyes closed revelling in the beautiful music.

Today, she decided, she was going in to see Jade.

About an hour later, she stood up and stretched her aching back and legs. She still didn't feel all that well, but she wasn't going to let that stop her going to the hospital. She made her way into the bedroom and got dressed.

Punch wasn't alert enough to escape her clutches, and it wasn't long afterwards that he found himself dumped unceremoniously into the laundry.

Ruby was at the hospital just over half an hour later.

***

Topaz and Pearl walked to the lift.

"I really don't like hospitals." Pearl noted. "The smell always reminds me of my past. So often I had to treat myself for the wounds your father inflicted. The antiseptic smell has always given me the willies."

Topaz was sympathetic.

"I wasn't sorry when he died," she said. "He was so cruel to you. I was scared of him, you know."

Pearl nodded.

"So was I! The only thing that kept me going was that he never hit you. I had to stop him when you were young, grab you and get you away. It always meant I got hit harder, though."

"Gosh, Mum, I'm so sorry!"

"No matter," Pearl said. "At least, for a few years, after your tenth birthday, he seemed to calm down a bit, although it never stopped, and I was always scared it would be worse every time he came home."

Topaz was saved from saying more when the lift door opened and they stepped out near Jade's room.

When they turned into room fifteen they were surprised to see both Jewel and David there.

Topaz smiled.

"Hello you two." David and Jewel turned to look at them. Topaz continued. "My, don't you look good," This was said to Jade with a smile.

David stood.

"I'll leave you for a while," he said. "The staff don't like too many in here at one time. I'll go for a walk." He kissed Jade on the forehead and squeezed her hand. "I'll be back soon."

As soon as he had gone, Jade spoke. "Where's Saffy?" Her voice was soft and weak.

Topaz didn't quite know what to say. Jewel spoke.

"I guess she's a little upset still," she said to Jade. "I saw her just after the accident. She told me that you were here, then she disappeared off to do something for her mother." She turned to Topaz. "Is she alright? It must have been a shock for her."

Topaz smiled a little distractedly.

"Mmm, I guess so. I'll talk to you in a little while about that."

At that moment Ruby entered the room.

"Oh," she stopped.

Jade looked at her with a frown.

"Do I know you?" she asked.

Everyone turned to look at her with the same question reflected in their eyes.

Ruby blushed.

"Um! I helped at the park." She mumbled.

"Pardon?" Jewel asked.

"I saw the accident, helped Jade and got Saffy to call the ambulance." She said a little louder. "Look, I'll leave – sorry to interrupt, I just wanted to see how Jade was."

Jewel stood and put her arm around Ruby's shoulder and led her to the bed.

"No way. You come over and join us. I'm really pleased to meet you. You mustn't feel that you are in the way. Without you, we have no way of knowing what would have happened to Jade. I remember you being here when I first arrived. I wondered who you were then. Now that I know, I need to say - thank you so much!"

She pulled up the chair next to the bed and helped Ruby into it.

Everyone agreed, and even Jade thanked her.

"I vaguely remember being rather rude to you," she said.

Ruby shook her head. "Don't worry about that – just get better – that's all I want."

After a little while Pearl spoke.

"How about you and I go and have a coffee, Ruby. I think there are too many people here and it's tiring Jade."

Topaz agreed. "I might come down soon, too. It will give us a chance to get to know Ruby. Perhaps she can shed some light on what might have happened to Saffy. I'm getting terribly worried. As soon as we leave here we must get out there and search."

Pearl nodded. "Perhaps Jade can give us a few clues?"

Jewel shook her head.

"No. I don't think that's wise yet. Jade needs to get well."

"I think I'll come down with you after all," Topaz said to Ruby and Pearl. She went over to Jade and gave her a careful hug, and a kiss. Turning to Jewel she spoke softly.

"If there's anything we can do, just let me know."

Jewel clutched her hand and squeezed. "Absolutely" she said. "I think we'll all need as much support as we can give each other. Please let me know when you find Saffy, too."

" Yes," she nodded. "I'm anxious to find her. It's not like her to disappear. Even when she was in the midst of her depression, she was always at home." Topaz turned and spoke to Jade. "We'll come back in a little while. Enjoy the visit with your mother. We'll come back and say bye when we've finished our coffee."

They all left the room. From the end of the corridor where he had been pacing backwards and forwards, David saw them leave. He went back to be with Jewel and give her his support. He was beginning to think of Jewel and Jade as 'his two girls'. The thought flashed through his mind that he had better not get too close in case the new relationship he had with Jewel might not last. He pushed the thought away. The women needed him at the moment, and he would do his best for them. If things didn't work out later, he'd face the problem then.

***

At the hospital cafeteria the group found a table. Topaz suggested that Ruby and Pearl sit down and she went over to the counter to order their drinks.

Ruby sat quietly, not quite knowing what to say.

Pearl spoke first. "Thanks, Ruby. It was good of you to help Jade."

Ruby looked embarrassed. "Please," she implored. "No more. Anyone would have done what I did. I just happened to be the first one there!"

Pearl smiled. "I guess so." she hesitated, then continued. "By the way, do you come from Germany? I seem to recognise the accent."

"Yes, as a matter of fact. I grew up on the outskirts of Stuttgart."

"That's amazing!" Pearl said with delight. "I was adopted and lived in Munich in my youth."

By the time Topaz came back to the table, the two older women were chatting about Germany as if they'd known each other all their lives.

***

After lunch Saffy watched Rod. He was getting ready to go to work.

"Why are you going in so early today?" Saffy asked.

"The boss wants me to do some cleaning up and prepping. He has a large group of people booked in tonight. I think he's panicking!"

Saffy was pleased, but she didn't show it. It would mean she had daylight to find her next accommodation. She was scared inside as well. Leaving the security that Rod had given her was difficult, but she just couldn't risk it anymore. If the police got wind of his drug supplying, she would be a goner as well.

"Besides – I need the money that comes with the overtime." Rod added. "I still won't be home till around midnight or later. Will you be OK?"

Saffy nodded. She didn't trust herself to speak.

As soon as Rod left, Saffy began to gather her few possessions. She crammed them into her backpack, then hastily scribbled a note, telling Rod thanks, but no thanks. She left the studio only about half an hour after he had gone.

Once she was back out on the street all the doubts came back. She imagined everyone was watching her, that police were around the next corner waiting for her, that she had a huge arrow pointing at her from the skies. She knew logically that this was not the case, but it didn't matter what she told herself, the feeling wouldn't go away.

She walked into the local supermarket, and wandered along the aisles. Every now and again she pocketed something to eat that was small enough not to be noticed. By the time she went to leave, she was looking over her shoulder in case she was being followed. When she was out in the street again without anyone accosting her, she felt uncomfortably victorious. She tried to appear nonchalant, sauntering passed several shops and around a corner before she broke into a run and fled the area.

When she stopped to take a breath, she realised she was in the vicinity of Rod's place again. Just then a shower of rain forced her to duck into the alcove of a café. She stood, wondering what to do next when she became aware of the conversation of two elderly women sitting nearby having a bite to eat.

"Have you heard?" The one with her hair up in a bun spoke conspiratorially to the other woman who was about to take a bite from a scone lathered with jam and whipped cream.

"What?" She lowered the scone a little and looked at the lady with the lavender scarf and the glasses perched on the end of her nose.

"There's been a murder near here, and the murderer got away."

"You don't say! What happened?" Her eyes sparkled with the joy of the gossip. Then she took a large bite of the bun. Cream oozed out of each side of her mouth.

"Not real sure," the friend replied. "But I hope they throw the book at her when they find her!"

"The murderer was a woman?" She grabbed a serviette and daintily wiped the cream off her mouth.

"So I believe," replied her friend.

"Why do they think that?"

"Well, I'm not sure."

By then Saffy was stunned and scared. She didn't want to hear anymore. She bolted out of the protection of the niche and out into the rain. She dashed to the stairwell and galloped up the steps, two at a time, back into Rod's studio.

She sat in what she considered was her beanbag, shivering and soaked through, for nearly an hour. At last she had calmed down enough to relax. In fact, she was still there when Rod came home.

She had fallen asleep, and the first thing that registered was Rod shaking her.

She awoke to a piece of paper being waved in front of her face.

"What is the meaning of this, Saffy?"

She clenched her teeth and her fists! Damn! She had forgotten to get rid of the note!

She flung out her hand and grabbed the note, shredding it.

"Nothing!" she snapped. "Nothing! I just got the willies and was going to leave."

"Why?" Rod asked, amazed. "You couldn't be safer than here!"

Saffy didn't really know what to tell him. She didn't want him to get any angrier. She decided honesty was the best policy.

"Well – it was the drug thing," she squeaked.

"What?" Rod looked at her in confusion.

""I thought the police might come and ask you questions if they figured out you were drug trafficking!"

Rod rocked back on his heels, sat down in the other beanbag and looked at Saffy. She was still half-asleep, her eyes puffy and her hair tangled. Then he did something she didn't expect.

He started to laugh.

The longer she stared at him with accusation in her eyes, the longer and louder he laughed.

Finally Saffy couldn't stand it any longer.

"Well?" she said with a whine in her voice. "What did you expect me to think?"

Rod calmed down.

"Goodness, Saffy. I don't make a habit of it! I'd hidden the joints so no one else would find them. I didn't think you would! I was only joking about selling them – I don't smoke at all. They are Roger's from down the street." Rod was still highly amused and stopped to catch his breath as he explained. "He smokes, left them here one night a couple of weeks ago and I was going to get them to him when I could. The night he forgot 'em, he was so off his face, he wasn't even aware he'd even rolled 'em. They were still on the floor when I woke up the next morning. I'd reckon he doesn't even know about them, so no harm done!"

It took some time before they both settled. Rod pushed himself up from the beanbag and went and made himself something to eat. Saffy cuddled down and tried to go back to sleep.

In the end, Rod came over to her and slipped under the blanket onto her beanbag, put his arms around her. Cuddled together they both finally slid into dreamland.

13.

Jewel and David sat with Jade for a little while longer. At one point, Jade asked about Saffy once again. Jewel explained that she hadn't spoken to Topaz yet, so when she had she would let her know. Perhaps, she suggested, Saffy was uncomfortable coming to a hospital as it wasn't anybody's favourite place! Jade was still feeling a little confused and asked if she was at school. Jewel looked at David and raised her eyebrows.

"No, Honey. It's holidays at present."

Eventually Jewel noticed that Jade's eyes were having trouble staying open, and she stopped talking. Slowly Jade's breathing settled into a quiet rhythm and David patted Jewel on the shoulder.

"Come on," he whispered. "Let her sleep. We'll come back again tomorrow."

In the car park a little later, Jewel turned to David.

"Do you think she's going to get any better?" she asked. There was a tremor in her voice as she looked up at him with a concerned question in her eyes.

David pointed the keys at the doors and unlocked them with a push of a button. He put his arm around Jewel's back and led her to the car, opening the door and helping her inside.

"Sweetheart," he squatted down and looked into her eyes. "Jade is doing very well. She is nearly back to her old self. I think she'll be back home before you know it."

***

While the two older women were talking, Topaz suggested that she would go back up to Jade's room, as she wanted to speak to Jewel.

Perhaps Jade may be able to give her some clues to the whereabouts of her daughter.

However, when she got there, Jewel and David had already gone, and Jade was fast asleep.

She went back to the café.

"Well, Jewel and David have gone." She said as she slid into the seat next to Pearl and across from Ruby.

"I wish they had let us know, but I guess they are too pre-occupied to think to let us know what's happening with Jade." She sighed.

Pearl patted her on the hand.

"Stop worrying," she said. "Jade will be OK – she already looked pretty good, I thought."

"Yes, but…"

"I know," Pearl interrupted, while Ruby took the last drink from her mugaccino. "You thought maybe she could help you find Saffy."

Topaz nodded.

"Listen, love. Saffy's a big girl. She'll come home when she's ready." Topaz looked sceptical at that comment from her mother. Pearl continued. "I think she was probably in shock and thinks the worse about Jade's condition."

"Perhaps you're right." Topaz agreed.

"Of course I'm right, dear," Pearl said, looking at Ruby for confirmation.

Ruby nodded in Topaz's direction, then stood up.

"Ladies, I'm sorry, but I'm going to have to go home. I've got my poor cat locked in the laundry and he hates it!"

Topaz stood up immediately. She noticed that Ruby was looking a little pale.

"By all means Ruby. You look tired. Do you want me to take you home?"

Ruby declined.

"No, No. I don't want you to go to any trouble."

"No trouble," Topaz said briskly. She turned to Pearl. "Come on Mum, let's get Ruby home. We'll pick you up again tomorrow, and we'll all come in together again."

She took absolutely no notice of Ruby when she tried to tell her that she would be fine going home on the bus.

Soon they were in Topaz's car and on their way.

***

The pattern of the next few days consisted of a visit to the hospital, picking up Ruby on the way. Each day they had a coffee in the café. Each day they met Jewel and David. Each day they became better and better friends, and each day Jade asked about Saffy. No one had heard any more from her, and eventually they had to tell Jade that Saffy was missing.

That day Jade cried and cried. They all worried in case the news would cause her to relapse, but slowly and surely Jade's health improved.

Some two weeks after the accident, Jade was discharged from the hospital.

***

By that stage Ruby was exhausted. She was actually relieved as well, as Topaz had not listened when Ruby had said she didn't need to go in to the hospital every day. When the visits stopped, Ruby slept for a whole day.

Punch pummelled her occasionally as he tried to get more comfortable on the bed, but Ruby didn't stir. When she did awake, Punch wasn't impressed. She was forgetting to feed him, and, in fact, herself as well.

Ruby staggered out to the kitchen, made a cup of tea, and went straight back to bed. She couldn't believe she was so tired.

***

Pearl and Topaz were really worried about Saffy, as there was still no communication from her apart from the first hurried message on the answering service. Topaz had not gone back to *'The Blue Stocking'* even though Gus had rung several times. She kept putting him off with excuses about having to visit Jade, and then her concerns about Saffy. Pearl was still staying with her, and this was beginning to get on her nerves as well. Each day they got into the car a drove around and around the area, looking for signs of Saffy. Occasionally, Topaz would stop and duck into a shop with a picture of her daughter, asking the people behind the counter if there had been any sightings. So far they had had no luck.

Two days after Jade had gone home, Topaz suggested to her mother that they go around and visit Ruby.

"Now that we have met her, and she is so alone, I think it would be nice to keep up the relationship," she said.

Pearl agreed, so they got ready and were soon on their way.

Topaz knocked at the front door and stood waiting on the little porch, noticing as she did so that the cane furniture really needed throwing away. Cobwebs festooned the window surrounds, and everything was grey with dust.

When there was no answer, Pearl told Topaz she was going around the back to check that everything was OK.

Pearl disappeared and Topaz waited.

The front door opened and Topaz got a shock to see her mother.

"Ruby left the back door unlocked, and she's in bed asleep," whispered Pearl. "I think we should help her out here – I don't think she's fed herself, or the cat, for two days!"

Topaz entered the house. The smell of cat was overpowering, and when they walked into the kitchen, there was no food in the cat's bowl, and no dishes in the sink except for a stained and chipped mug.

Topaz checked the cupboards and put down some food for the cat. It had come out to see what was going on, and was meowing pitifully at them.

Then Pearl made a cup of tea and crept into the small bedroom.

"Ruby?"

Ruby stirred.

"Ruby," Pearl said again a little louder.

Ruby opened her eyes. She didn't seem at all surprised to see Pearl in her room. She sat up slowly as Pearl placed the tea on the bedside table, then perched on the side of Ruby's bed.

"You OK?" she asked.

Ruby smiled and then yawned.

"I'm just so tired!" she remarked. "But I'm OK. Thanks so much for the tea. How long have you been here?"

"Not long," Pearl smiled. "We couldn't wake you up when we knocked. Hope you don't mind – we came in the back door – it was unlocked."

Pearl was concerned. Ruby was pale, and yet her eyes had bags under them and her cheeks looked sunken.

Ruby picked up the cup of tea, and as she drank, the colour began to return to her face.

Pearl stood up.

"Topaz is here, too. We'll go out into the lounge and wait for you to get out of bed." Pearl walked to the door. "Or would you prefer that we went?"

"No, no." Ruby shook her head. "I'll be out in a minute. Make yourself at home."

It was about fifteen minutes later that Ruby came in to the lounge. She had wrapped herself in her pink dressing gown. It had seen better days, and Ruby looked the same. She seemed to be smaller than Pearl and Topaz remembered, and she was slightly stooped.

Ruby made her way to the altar and she stopped and looked at the photos. She reached up and caressed the photo of her husband, and then she turned and sat down on her favourite armchair.

"Aah, girls," she murmured. "I wish you could have met my Joseph."

Topaz looked at Pearl and raised her eyebrows quickly.

Pearl spoke.

"He looks as if he was a lovely man."

Ruby smiled.

Over another cup of tea, the three women talked and talked.

Pearl and Ruby had so much in common.

They talked about Germany, and how Pearl had run away from her adoptive parents, and how Saffy had now followed the same path.

Suddenly Ruby brightened.

"Pearl?' she said, her voice quivering with a quiet excitement. "Do you think…?"

Pearl looked at her with her own questions in her eyes.

"What, Ruby?" she asked quietly.

"Do you think you might be my daughter?"

Topaz gasped.

***

Saffy was sick of the studio. She hadn't been outside again since her abortive attempt to flee. She was suffering from 'cabin fever' Rod laughingly told her.

"Get out and do something," he said. "You've been cooped up here for nearly a fortnight."

Saffy flexed her shoulders and agreed.

"There have been no police asking questions – and I think you heard those ladies talking about the problem that had occurred in Redfern. It was a domestic, and the woman was found – she was suffering more wounds than the man she'd stabbed!"

Sapphire sighed and shrugged.

"I should really find a job," she said. "I've been bludging on you too long now."

Rod laughed. "You've paid in other ways!" he teased, wriggling his eyebrows up and down.

Saffy blushed. Losing her virginity on a beanbag was not quite how she had expected it to happen. Now sex was a regular occurrence when Rod was around. They were finding it hard to keep their hands off of each other!

The subject was allowed to drop, and Saffy sat down and stared at the walls, while Rod put his arms around her. Rod kissed her on the back of the neck, running his hands over her breasts. She moaned, and turned towards him.

Before too long, Rod had found his supply of condoms and Saffy was spread-eagled on the beanbag again. They made love with wild abandon, passion born of youth, inexperience and the glory of new love.

Afterwards they stayed cuddled together until Rod finally broke the mood.

"It's no use," he said sadly. "I can't stay like this – I've got to go to work."

Saffy grinned. She wrapped her legs around him.

"I'm not letting you go!" She ran her hands over his body and tightened her thighs.

Rod's eyes glazed over, but he grabbed her hand. "Stop, Saff! I really have to go!"

Saffy pretended offence, but she released her grip and turned over.

As he struggled to stand up, she looked up at him, and caressed his form with her eyes. Meeting Rod in front of the church those few short weeks ago had turned out far better than she could have imagined. She snuggled down again. In the afterglow of their lovemaking she decided that she would take the plunge this afternoon and go and look for work.

The fear of the police was slowly abating and she also thought she should go and find Ruby and find out just what had happened.

She sat upright suddenly!

"Oh!"

Rod came out of the toilet and looked at her.

"Anything wrong?" he asked

"No!" Saffy said. "I've just remembered! She said 'the one with the purple door'."

"Who said?" Rod was curious.

"It doesn't matter," Saffy climbed out of the beanbag. "I've just decided – I'm going out! I'll see you tonight when you come home from work!" and then she reached for her jeans and got dressed.

Rod frowned, but Saffy would say no more.

***

An hour later, Saffy was sauntering down Cleveland Street as if she didn't have a care in the world. However, she looked at each of the terrace houses as she passed, until a purple door suddenly seemed to glow, and all the other houses faded into a blur.

She stopped.

The doubts came back with a rush. Should she go in? What if they were waiting for her to make this move? What if Ruby dobbed her in? What if… What if…

She turned and walked over to the park and sat down heavily on one of the benches under the trees. She kept looking at the purple door, but she didn't move. At one point she saw her mother and Oma come along the road in Topaz's car. She shrank down, feeling concealed by the tree, and watched. The car disappeared and when it appeared again, Saffy could see Ruby in the car as well. She wondered what was happening. How had her Mother and Oma met Ruby? Were they looking for her? Had they seen Jade's mother? Was there any ongoing search?

Eventually she walked slowly back to Rod's studio. She hadn't had the courage to wait and find out if they returned. The only consolation was that now she knew where Ruby lived.

***

David had meanwhile gone back to work at the real estate office. In order to look after Jade, Jewel had taken her holidays.

It was nothing short of a miracle, as far as David was concerned, that their relationship had continued to flourish, and there had been no return to the hard and selfish Jewel of the past.

Every evening he went around to Jewel's place and checked that all was well, often taking in a Chinese takeaway meal so that he felt as if he was contributing to the rehabilitation efforts for Jade.

Jade continued to improve, although it was very obvious that she mourned the absence of her friend.

"I'm sure Saffy is OK." Her mother told her. "I don't understand why she hasn't contacted or visited you, but there must be a good reason. You always did everything together and Saffy must be wondering how you are. You know we are keeping in touch with Jade's Mum and Grandmother. They go out every day looking for Saffy. Even Ruby has been helping."

Jade would nod, but Jewel despaired of the faraway look that would enter Jade's eyes when they spoke about Sapphire, or when Topaz or Pearl visited.

Ruby had also come and seen them a couple of times.

Jewel had commented to Topaz, that the older woman was not looking well, and yet there was something like hope glimmering in her eyes when she looked at Pearl.

Topaz told her why.

"Ruby's got it into her mind that Pearl is her long lost daughter," she explained. "I guess it's possible."

"Is that why Pearl has been doing more research into her past?" Jewel asked.

"Yes," Topaz answered. "It's pretty slow going though. The records for all the concentration camps were a bit light on real information. So many of them have disappeared, and the lists and numbers of people that were gassed are horrendous. I have wondered why they don't organise a DNA test?"

"I think that Pearl is too frightened to do that, in case it turns out they are not related! While there is no evidence, there is hope on both sides. After all they have already been through, I guess hope is a strong emotion." Jewel commented.

There was silence for a few moments, then Jewel added. "I can't believe all the trauma Ruby and your Mum have been through – I never knew! I know my life and probably yours, too, hasn't been a bed of roses – but war and the cruelties that were done to the people in the concentration and death camps was awful."

"I agree," Topaz said. "But, you know – war anywhere brings out the worst and best in people."

"I guess so," Jewel acknowledged. "But still..."

They both stopped and looked at the women around them. Jade was still fragile, but coping, Pearl was hoping to find out about her mother and Ruby was hoping she would finally get confirmation that Pearl was her daughter. Topaz had finished her relationship with Gus and *'The Blue Stocking'* and looked happier than she had done for ages, although there was the underlying sadness for her lost daughter and she was also hoping her daughter would soon be home. Jewel was in a new relationship with David and was hoping her daughter would get better. She still couldn't believe the changes that the accident had caused. They had all become close, all become a family.

All that needed to occur now was bringing Saffy back into the fold. That would put the icing on the cake.

Over the next few days, whenever they visited Jade and Jewel, their friendships deepened. Slowly the barriers each woman had erected around herself to protect the hurts inside were beginning to crumble.

14.

Jewel was the first one to break down.

David was visiting, and Jade had gone to sleep.

They were sitting quietly on the sofa, drinking a relaxing glass of Merlot, when David asked. "Jewel, you never mention your past. Are your parents still around?"

Jewel was silent for some time, and David thought she hadn't heard him. He put down his glass and turned to say it again when he caught his breath. Tears were running down Jewel's face.

"Oh, Jewel, I'm sorry," he moved towards her, but she shook her head.

"No," she sobbed. "It's OK."

"I didn't mean to upset you."

"I didn't mean to break down, either," she sighed. "The stress with Jade has just been too much."

"I understand," David agreed, taking the wine from her hand and putting it on the coffee table.

As her put his arms around her, she turned into the warmth of his chest and he felt her shoulders shake as more sobs made her hiccup. When she could calm herself a little, it all poured out.

"Mum and Dad did nothing but criticise me," she said between sobs. "I tried so hard, but they never praised me. In the end I thought they hated me. Nothing ever went right, and then … then …they were killed in a car accident and I was left all alone."

David waited, not saying a word, but in his mind it all began to make sense.

"I never got to tell them that I passed my end of school exams with distinctions." She took a ragged breath and continued. "I decided there and then that I would prove to them, even though they were gone, and myself, that I was better than anyone else."

David nodded, and patted her back. He could feel the material of his shirt sticking to his skin as her tears soaked through.

"I just worked and worked – I met my husband and had Jade, but I couldn't stand the solitude – I had to go back to work. He never understood – he harped and harped at me – he wanted a little uncomplaining woman who slaved away in the kitchen, being there to deliver his every need – until I left, taking Jade with me. The divorce wasn't pleasant – I got nothing except custody of Jade – the judge said I could give her more than him – he wasn't earning nearly as much as me." She gulped and sobbed between each comment. "I took that as the spur to work even harder - I hated the dependence I felt when I was married, so I just covered up my hurts with a hard shell – and I used man after man – to prove I could."

She took a breath and David made soothing sounds in her ear. He loved that she was telling him all of this. He loved the smell of her, and the tickle of her hair on his neck.

"I'm so sorry." She continued before David could say anything. "Before the accident I could hear Jade doing the same as I did when I was young. She asked and asked for my approval, but I was cold to her pleas. Now I don't know whether she will ever be able to do anything again. I should have been more supportive. I'm scared now I'll be trapped looking after her – never being able to be a person in my own right again. Am I awful to think that way? What am I going to do? I am so sorry I used you David. Can you forgive me? Can Jade forgive me? Can I forgive me?" she hiccoughed and tried to laugh at herself, but it ended up in a strangled cry.

David just held her.

That night, David stayed. They slept curled up together. There was tenderness, cuddles and more tears from Jewel, but David was glad she didn't want sex. She didn't use him, and didn't abuse his body. The love of acceptance from David was all she needed.

She began, that night, to heal.

The next morning, over breakfast, Jade wandered out as David was hugging her mother. They sprung apart as if their skin was suddenly on fire. They didn't know what Jade's reaction would be. Jewel thought that Jade blamed her for the break down of the marriage, and that she still loved her father.

Jade smiled shyly.

"Finally you two decided to get together," she said, and Jewel visibly relaxed. "I just wish you'd been able to feel that for Dad. By the way, why didn't you let him know about my accident?" Jewel pursed her lips and raised her eyes to the ceiling. Jade frowned. "I would have liked him visiting me. He's going to be hurt. I really miss both him and Saff. I wish…" She looked confused again, and Jewel left David's side and came over to her.

"Sorry, Honey." She handed her the cordless phone off of the kitchen bench. "You know I can't talk to him – but you should ring him." She looked at the clock. "He'll still be home – he doesn't leave for his work for another half an hour."

Jade took the phone, pushed a couple of buttons and when he answered, she walked out of the room, went to the lounge and curled up on the sofa to chat for the next fifteen minutes.

David raised an eyebrow.

"You OK?" he asked

Jewel shrugged. "I will be," she said and turned and made coffee for them both.

***

Pearl spoke to Topaz over her bowl of Weetbix and milk.

"I'm wondering whether I should go home?"

"No way, Mum," Topaz said quickly. "That would be like giving up on Sapphire."

"Well, I don't know what I can do," Pearl added. "The police were no help when you went to the station to report her missing."

"Tell me about it," Topaz agreed. She put on a sour face and said in a deep voice. "Sorry, Ma'am. There's nothing we can do. She's allowed to leave home at her age. Besides she should be missing more than twenty-four hours anyway."

"Well, you can't blame him," Pearl said. "I don't think he was very impressed when you told him she'd been missing for three days and you hadn't noticed!"

Topaz put her elbows on the table and held her head as she nodded. She looked up at her mother with sigh.

"Please don't go yet," she implored. "We've got to try and find Saffy and get her to come home. I'm still at a loss to figure out why she has disappeared like this. If she hadn't rung and told us she was safe I would be out of mind imagining her lying dead somewhere – although every day I still see that in my mind." She stopped and raised her hands to an invisible God. "I just wish I knew where she was!"

"Ok," Pearl surrendered. "I understand. I wish I knew what was going on with her, too. She always used to tell me all her troubles. I don't know why she hasn't this time!"

"Maybe she has tried!" Topaz said emphatically. "You haven't been home, you know, and you haven't got a mobile! What if she's been at your place all this time?"

"Perhaps so!" Pearl said. "That's a good reason for me to go home!"

"Yeah! You're right," Topaz said, as she turned to put the dishes on the sink. "By the way – what sort of troubles would she want to unload onto you and not me?"

Pearl took a deep breath. "I don't want to tell stories out of school, but I guess the main one was the way she felt about not knowing who her father was."

Topaz bit her lip and turned away, staring at the froth of soap in the sink. There was no way she was going to let that particular cat out of the bag. To this day, she still remembered the hurt that her father had caused to her mind and her body. He didn't care what he did to her, just as long as she spread her legs and he got his jollies. Sometimes, when he was so drunk that he couldn't get it up, he had forced her to suck him, until he had come in her mouth. When she retched, he had laughed as he pulled up his trousers. She felt tears well up in her eyes.

She put her hand up and swiped at her eyes. She turned back to Pearl.

"Well that's one thing I'll think about telling her when I finally get her home. After I've hugged her, of course, then yelled at her for putting us through this worry!"

"Good!" said Pearl, looking at Topaz searchingly.

Topaz knew she was angling to be told, too. She ignored the hint.

"Let's go out and have a wander around the shops this morning," she said, swallowing the lump in her throat that the memories had caused, and plastering a smile on her face.

Pearl got up.

"OK. But it'll be a miracle if you catch sight of Saffy in the shops."

She walked out to get ready, and Topaz had to admit that she was only going out for that very reason.

***

Ruby made herself a cup of tea, fed Punch and took the mug back into the bedroom. She didn't feel quite right this morning.

Again.

She just couldn't seem to keep her eyes open for long. Her energy levels were so low, that even getting up had been a struggle.

She shuffled back to bed and got under the covers. She plumped up the pillows behind her and waited until Punch had jumped up and settled himself before she picked up the mug and took a sip.

She noticed her hands shook a little, and carefully replaced the mug on the bedside table.

"Well, Punch. I think I've found my daughter! Isn't that great?"

Punch took absolutely no notice; he was already comfortable and asleep.

"You naughty boy!" she said to the cat, without too much conviction. "You always ignore me! Anyway, you're not supposed to be on the bed."

She reached out her hand and stroked him. He began to purr and Ruby smiled. Punch stayed exactly where he was, and Ruby let him.

She snuggled down and slept for the next four hours.

***

When she awoke she struggled out of bed, as she needed to respond to the call of nature. Punch never moved.

By the time she had got up, made her way to the bathroom, and begun to return to her room, her energy had run out. She put her hand out to the sideboard in the lounge in order to steady herself. She got no further. Her legs gave out and she quietly crumpled to the floor. There was no way that she was going to move for some time. She closed her eyes.

15.

When Rod had left, Saffy was still feeling some sexual energy after the hectic and fervent lovemaking. She got up and had a relaxing, hot shower.

Once she was dressed in casual clothes, she took a deep breath and hurried down the stairs and out of the studio.

She made her way straight to Cleveland Street and the purple door. It had haunted her for days. She stood outside the gate and looked at it. Would she go in today? Would Ruby welcome her? Why had she come?

She turned away, still lacking the courage to go further.

"This is silly," she thought. *"I can't go on like this. I'll never be able to face her if I don't do it now."*

Not thinking of the consequences, she immediately turned back, opened the gate, made her way to the front door and knocked.

What had she done?

What would she say?

Should she run?

She stood, hesitating, on the porch. The cane furniture looked dirty. The cobwebs moved faintly in the breeze. The traffic on the street continued to flow.

The door, however, remained closed.

Saffy decided that Ruby wasn't home. She backed down the steps towards the front gate, constantly watching the purple door.

Nothing.

No sounds.

Saffy walked away.

Before she could go further, her conscience niggled.

Maybe…?

No! What was she thinking?

If she went around the back, Ruby might be outside in the garden. She should take the plunge. She really needed to talk to Ruby. She needed to find out whether she had talked to the police. She needed to tell her not to if she hadn't already done so.

She gritted her teeth, clenched her fists and walked up the alleyway behind the terrace houses, pushing open the back gate of the fourth yard along, and stepped into the neglected garden. She strode up to the back door before she could change her mind.

Her courage began to seep away. She knocked timidly on the door and waited.

Once again there was no response.

She tried the door handle, and the door opened.

A large tortoiseshell cat stalked to the door and looked at Saffy, meowing loudly.

"Sssh!" Saffy glared at the animal. "What's wrong with you?" she hissed.

The cat continued to yowl then moved away, stopping and looking back at her.

Saffy tiptoed into the room.

She saw an arm and hand stretched out on the floor. For one horrible moment she stood, terrified.

Then thoughts rushed into the void.

"Oh my God – she's dead! I should go! I don't want to look. Now she'll never tell. God, I'm selfish. Maybe I can help? No! I can't, I can't, I should! I must!"

As the thoughts tumbled around, her feet crept forward.

She shut her eyes tight, but couldn't help herself – she opened them again, reluctantly, and looked around the doorjamb and saw Ruby on the ground.

"Oh! My! God!"

All the fears and doubts flew away. She raced over and squatted beside her.

Ruby slowly opened her eyes. She moaned.

"I'll ring the ambulance," Saffy consoled her. She stood and looked around for a phone.

"No phone," Ruby croaked.

Saffy gasped.

"Oh! Ruby! I haven't got one either. I'll have to leave you so I can find a phone!"

Ruby nodded carefully with small painful movements.

"I know, Saffy," she whispered. "Now it's your turn to help me."

"I will! Stay where you are." She winced when she realised what she'd said, but continued quickly. "I'll be back!"

She raced out of the back door, through the gate, down the alleyway and along the street. There wasn't a public phone in sight. She dashed into the first shop she saw.

"Can I use your phone?" she gasped, holding her side and trying to catch her breath. "I need to call an ambulance."

The lady behind the counter didn't say a word – she passed Saffy the cordless from the wall.

After she had let them know the details of her need, she handed the phone back and ran out of the shop, shouting out a 'thank you' over her shoulder. She was back sitting beside Ruby before she'd had time to register what she had done.

Ruby's eyes fluttered open and she peered up and saw Saffy. She smiled when Saffy patted her arm.

"I've called the ambulance – they'll be here soon."

"Thank you," Ruby whispered weakly. "You're a good girl. Without you, Jade wouldn't have been home today – now you're helping me." Her voice faded and her eyes closed.

In the silence, Saffy blinked. All she could hear was 'Jade' and 'home' running around and around.

Jade wasn't dead!

After all this time of fear and worry!

Jade wasn't dead!

Jade wasn't dead!

The stress fell from her like a waterfall. The relief was so strong she almost passed out. She could go home! Her mother and grandmother must be beside themselves with worry! What had she done? How could she fix this?

The siren of the ambulance hadn't penetrated, but the pounding on the front door registered. She jumped up and opened the door.

The ambulance officer entered the room, and she took over. Ruby was on the stretcher and in the vehicle quickly and calmly.

The officer turned to Saffy.

"Would you like to come with us?"

"No." Saffy murmured. "I have to let people know."

"I understand," the woman said.

Saffy knew the ambo had no way of understanding her situation at all. However, she gave the lady her information and asked her to tell Ruby she would be in to visit her as soon as possible.

***

Later that day, Topaz was in the garden when she heard the phone ring. She very nearly didn't get inside in time to pick it up. She reached it on about the sixth ring.

"Hello," she said somewhat wearily.

"Mum?" The tentative little voice sent shock waves through Topaz's body.

"Darling!" she exclaimed. "Are you OK? Where are you?"

"Can I come home?" Saffy asked tremulously.

"Of course," Topaz tried very hard to keep the excitement out of her voice. She didn't want to scare her daughter away. "I'll be waiting. Can you get here yourself, or do you want me to come and get you?"

But she was talking to empty air. Saffy had already hung up.

***

"Mum!" Topaz yelled as she put the phone down. "That was Saffy! She's coming home!"

Pearl looked up from her research on the computer and almost cheered.

"That's wonderful!" she exclaimed. "Did she tell you where she was? What did she say?"

Topaz calmed a little. "Actually she didn't say anything – just asked if she could come home."

"When?" Pearl asked.

"I don't know," Topaz excitement had now deflated. "She hung up on me!"

"Oh!" Pearl looked back at the computer screen. There was silence for a couple of moments, and Topaz bit her lip!

"You know, that could be good news," Pearl tried to brighten up again. "Maybe she's not far away!"

Topaz nodded.

"That's it! Hopefully she'll be home for dinner tonight!"

Pearl agreed. Then she said, rather apologetically. "I think I've found what happened to my mother," she said.

"Oh?" Topaz was curious and she tried to look over Pearl's shoulder at the computer screen.

"It's not as good news as yours though," Pearl said. "I think she was sent to the gas chambers."

"Really? Are you sure?" Topaz looked concerned.

"Well, no ... but ..."

Suddenly they were interrupted by a knock on the front door.

"Do you think that's...?" Topaz frowned, hesitating.

Her mother pushed her. "Go!"

She went to the door, and when she opened it she was delighted to see Saffy standing there.

She had a backpack slung over her shoulder, and her clothes were crumpled and dirty.

"Why did you knock?"

Saffy hung her head and looked at her shoes. "I didn't know if I'd be welcome!"

Topaz simply put out her arms and Saffy walked into them. The hug was long and warm and Saffy and Topaz both began to cry. Pearl came up behind them and gently moved them inside and shut the door. She stood back and watched the reunion, happy that it had ended so well. Recriminations would come later.

Within three seconds, Saffy was pushing away from her mother.

"Mum, listen."

Topaz held her still, resisting the ability for Saffy to step back. "Please listen, you need to know something." Saffy said again.

Pearl and Topaz looked at her.

"Mum, Ruby's in hospital. Is Jade really OK?"

Topaz frowned. "What do you mean?" She continued to look puzzled. "Of course Jade's OK! You saw her go in the ambulance – it was Jade that went to hospital, not Ruby!"

Saffy shook her head. "No! You don't understand! I thought Jade was…" she could say no more, but she drew up self up again then added. "I've just been around to Ruby's – I had to get the ambulance for her – she'd collapsed on the floor! I was so scared!"

"Really?" Pearl interrupted. "How did you know where Ruby lived? Did you realise we knew Ruby? Have you been watching us? Why haven't you contacted us?" There was a strange look of disbelief on her face. Pearl was still having a hard time coping with the knowledge that her mother was probably among the people gassed by the Nazis. She also wondered whether Saffy was lying, just to get out of answering questions about her disappearance.

Saffy turned to her.

"Oma – I love you, but it's a long story. I'll tell you later. But you need to know. When I went over to her place I found her on the floor! I was so scared, but I found a shop with a phone and called the ambulance for her." She stood and stared at her grandmother, her eyes showing Pearl that there was concern and sadness radiating from them.

Topaz didn't hesitate. She took charge.

"Well, come on you two. No use standing around. Let's get ready and go to the hospital. Ruby must have exhausted herself. She hasn't been looking well for ages. She needs our support after the way she helped Jade. I'll let Jewel and Jade know as well."

About three-quarters of an hour later they were sitting in traffic and Topaz was drumming her fingers on the steering wheel.

"Come on, come on." She muttered to the cars in front. "I haven't got all day!"

"It's OK, Mum." Saffy said from the back seat. "We'll get there in plenty of time."

Pearl turned and looked at her granddaughter.

"Yeah! I suppose they have to take her through the emergency department, and you know how long they take to do anything! Besides, I'd like to know a few things. Where have you been, and why the hell were you at Ruby's?"

"I don't want to talk about it now," Saffy turned away and looked out of the window towards the buildings, turning her back on her grandmother.

"Well, we're going to have to talk about it pretty damn soon!" Pearl was getting annoyed.

"Can we leave it for the moment, Mum?" Topaz turned her head and glared at her mother. "This isn't the time or the place. We have to think about Ruby now. Now that Saffy is home, she'll be able to sit down and tell us all in her own time." She smiled at Saffy. She still couldn't believe that her daughter was finally sitting next to her. In the back seat Pearl compressed her lips in frustration, but said no more.

The cars in front began to move as the traffic lights turned green and Topaz turned back as she concentrated on her driving.

Saffy sank back in the seat and sighed with relief. Now she began to worry about Jade and what had happened. She was also worried about Ruby, and to top off the problems, she had to get back to the studio and let Rod know what was going on. She hadn't thought to leave a note, just grabbed her backpack and sped home. Once again she hadn't stopped to think of the consequences of her actions.

After several more stops at traffic lights, the cars began to flow at a reasonable speed, and it wasn't long before they were looking for a park in the hospital parking area.

***

When Topaz rang Jewel and told her the news, Jewel immediately went in to see Jade.

"Do you remember the lady who helped you at the park?" she asked Jade.

Jade screwed up her face and thought.

"Ye..es. I think so!"

"I just got a call from Topaz. Saffy is home and said that the old lady was in hospital. Do you want to go in and see her?"

Jade nodded. Her face lit up. "Wonderful, Saffy is home. When can I see her?"

"You do realise we're going to see Ruby, not Saffy?"

"Yes," Jade said. "But I am so looking forward to seeing Saff. Where has she been?"

"I don't know," Jewel admitted. "Let's just take one step at a time. We'll go and see Ruby, then we'll go and see Topaz and Sapphire. OK?"

Jade nodded as she began to get ready to go out. There was a quiet excitement to her face, and Jewel was thrilled that her best friend had once again surfaced and that their friendship could continue. She wondered, of course, why Saffy had gone to ground, and she was anxious to find out, as she was sure Topaz and Pearl were, too.

Jewel went back to the phone and called David. She repeated the story.

"Do you think it is wise to take Jade?" David commented. "It might unsettle her again."

Jewel thought differently.

"I think it's a good idea," she answered. "It actually might help – give her some sort of closure."

"OK. I'll meet you there." David rang off.

***

Ruby was admitted to hospital soon after she arrived in the ambulance. In the emergency area, they had wired her up to monitors, and discovered, very quickly, that she'd suffered a heart attack, and she had been moved up to the heart ward promptly.

In the ward, nurses made her comfortable. She had several tubes attached, and the doctor had come and asked question after question. She couldn't stay awake, and she dozed off and on, while machines chirped around her, and nurses kept interrupting her to give her medication. They continuously seemed to be at her bedside taking readings of her vital signs.

Ruby knew that it wasn't the best she had ever been and she resigned herself to a long stay in hospital. She didn't know if she would go home soon, if ever, and she worried about Punch. No one talked to her, only *at* her, and she felt isolated and just a little frightened.

When Topaz stuck her head around the door, followed by Saffy and then Pearl, Ruby brightened considerably.

"They nearly didn't let us visit you," Topaz said by way of greeting. "I had to do some fast talking – so here we all are."

Ruby smiled weakly.

"Hello," she said, trying to sit up. "I'm so pleased to see you. Thank you Saffy for helping me. I'd been laying on the floor for ages."

Saffy smiled back at her.

"Don't try to sit up," she said quietly, then fussed with Ruby's pillows, making sure she was comfortable.

"I was better at making a decision for you than I was for Jade, she continued. "I just knew what I had to do – and your cat was stubborn and wouldn't let me go until I'd followed him!"

Ruby frowned.

"I'm worried about Punch. Will you check on him for me?"

Topaz laughed quietly. "We're all worried about *you*, Ruby! But yes! Of course we'll look after Punch. You have no need to worry - just get yourself better."

While they were speaking, Jewel and Jade walked in.

"Hi everybody. Hi Ruby."

Saffy immediately looked at Jade. There were several moments of silence, then the two girls embraced.

"I'm so pleased to see you, Jade." Saffy whispered in her ear.

"Same." Jade answered. "We must talk!" Saffy nodded and then they both went over to Ruby's bedside and gave her a careful hug, one on one side, and one on the other.

Ruby felt her heart swell with love for the two girls. Then she looked at Pearl. This was the best day of her life.

Here she was in a hospital bed, but now she had a family. Pearl smiled at her, then David walked in as well.

A nurse came bustling in.

"I didn't think this patient was allowed visitors," she said gruffly. "Sorry – everyone out. You can come back tomorrow if she is better – but only two people at a time please!"

Everyone began to go, with David bending over the old lady, kissing her soft and wrinkled cheek.

"Hurry up and get better," he said. "We can't wait for you to come back home and we can spoil you!"

When they had gone, Ruby closed her eyes and drifted back to sleep. There was a look of contentment on her face, almost a smile on her lips.

***

The group all went down stairs and by silent agreement made their way to the coffee lounge in the foyer.

They sat down and David organised their orders. While he was away at the counter, the girls began to talk. Jewel and Topaz looked on indulgently while Saffy and Jade chatted.

"It's so good to see Jade looking much more bright and healthy again," Jewel commented.

Pearl wasn't quite so happy. She wasn't looking at Jade.

"I would really like to sit down with that girl and find out what was going on in her mind to keep us all in such a state of worry," she said, staring at Saffy pointedly.

Topaz tried to shush her.

"We can talk later," she hissed at her mother, but by that time, Saffy had stopped talking and her eyes widened when she had heard her grandmother's comment. Silence fell over the small group.

"Don't you understand," Saffy said with a sob and a shake of her head. "I thought Jade was dead! I thought I'd killed my best friend!"

Jewel reached out and touched Saffy on her shoulder. Saffy flinched, not quite believing the softness of the touch from the woman that she had met out the front of the real estate office only such a short time ago. Jewel spoke.

"It must have been awful for you to think that. What *made* you think like that?"

Saffy shrugged. "It seems silly now, I guess." She said brokenly. "But all I saw was Jade being lifted into the ambulance and she wasn't moving. It was just like the day the ambulance came and took my girlfriend away at the other school all those years ago. I never saw her again, and I thought that I'd never see Jade again either!" She turned to Jade, breathed in a sob, then gave her another hug.

At that moment David came back to the table.

"Come on, everyone. Let's talk about this later, at home. I think Saffy wasn't thinking rationally because of the shock! Let's all give her the benefit of the doubt. You can clear everything up over the next few days. Now we have to think about Ruby and hope *she* gets better."

Pearl was belligerent.

"Yeah right! Are we all going to pretend that Saffy didn't put us through Hell? Do you think we should forget what happened?"

"No one said that, Mum." Topaz said. "We'll talk later – this isn't the time or place for this type of discussion. I told you that in the car. We'll find out and talk later."

The conversation lulled and everyone felt a little uncomfortable, so they finished their drinks and it wasn't long before Jewel got up.

"Come on, Jade." She put her hand out. Jade reluctantly stood up, reaching out to her Mum's hand. David got up and put his arm around Jewel and giving Jade a huge smile. "Come on, my sweet girls, let's go home."

Jewel glanced around at everyone. "Don't forget, you're all welcome to come around anytime. Saffy, I think Jade would like that, don't you?"

Saffy got up and hugged Jade again.

"Try and keep me away now" she said with determination.

They all dispersed.

16.

When they got home, Topaz called Pearl and Saffy and they all sat down in the lounge. She asked Saffy to explain what had happened.

Saffy went still and quiet.

"Listen, Mum. Can I tell you later? I've got something to do first."

"No." Pearl interrupted. "I'm fed up with all this. Tell your mother."

Saffy burst into tears.

Topaz went over and sat next to her, putting her arms around the girl.

"I'm sorry," she said.

Saffy lifted her head and looked at her mother with astonishment.

"Why, Mum. Why are you sorry?"

"Because I realise it's partly my fault. No!" she held up her hand as both Pearl and Saffy began to protest. "I have never been much of a mother to you – ignoring you while I put my time into my career."

"I always thought you hated me, you know." Saffy murmured.

Topaz looked at her mother then took a deep breath.

"You'd better both sit down and make yourselves comfortable. Before you go, Saffy, I think it's time I told the truth," she said.

**

"I think Jade is back to normal," Jewel said to David as they snuggled together in her bed.

"Mmm." David was still tired after the lovemaking just moments before. "Have you noticed that her memory isn't very good?"

"Yes," Jewel conceded. "But I think that will eventually get better."

David didn't answer. He was almost asleep.

Jewel extracted herself from his arms. When he murmured and tried to hold on, she gently pushed away. He turned over and his breathing became even as he fell into a deep sleep.

Jewel got up and slipped her silk house robe on, then padded on bare feet out into the kitchen.

She was surprised to see Jade already there.

Jade looked at her and smiled.

"It seems you and David have become a serious item since I had my accident!" she said.

"Yes," her mother agreed. She was happy Jade hadn't known about the sexual relationship that Jewel had had with David before. "Do you mind?"

"No, not at all," Jade grinned. "It has made you a much nicer person."

Jewel looked at her and raised her eyebrows. "Well, actually – it wasn't David that did that!" she said. "I realised how close I came to losing you when you had the fall, and I had been so caught up in proving myself, I forgot you needed support as well."

"Thanks, Mum." Jade came over to her and gave her a hug, and Jewel hugged back, something that she hadn't done for ages. It felt good.

"Can I go over and see Saffy today?" Jade asked.

"Sure," Jewel agreed. "But you'll have to wait until after we've visited Ruby."

Jade screwed up her face. "Nuuuh!" she whinged.

"Come on, Jade. You know that without her help you may not be standing here today! It's the least you can do. Besides – did you know? – she was the first person to sit with you in hospital?"

Jade shook her head. "Was she?"

Jewel nodded.

"Well … Yeah – I guess you're right. I'll go and get changed." Jade looked her mother up and down. "And I guess you'd better change, too. I think that's the first time ever I've seen you without your make-up and 'work' clothes – I like it! But I don't think you would be comfortable going out like that!"

Jewel smiled and patted her on the bottom as she walked away.

"Go on, then. I won't be far behind you – just got to wake up my sleeping Adonis in there!' and she inclined her head towards the bedroom.

Jade giggled.

***

Pearl sat and stared at Topaz. This couldn't be happening. Topaz had vowed and declared that she would *never* speak about the father of her daughter to *anyone*!

Topaz began.

"I have to admit – I never wanted to speak about this!"

Pearl blinked – she hadn't said that thought out aloud, surely.

"But I think we are all aware that something's got to be said." Topaz continued. She looked at Saffy, who was sitting quite still, looking at her mother with large expressive eyes.

"You know, Saffy – you were right. I didn't want you!" Saffy gulped, a sob torn from her throat. "But that didn't last for very long once I saw you." She sat down on the stool by the kitchen bench and took a deep breath. "You were conceived in less than ideal conditions. I found it hard to show my love for you, even when I felt it inside."

"Oh!" There was a sound of despair from Pearl. Topaz turned to her. "No! Mum, I wasn't raped – not once, but dozens of times."

Pearl frowned. 'I thought…"

"You probably didn't think of the actual truth, though." Topaz gathered her courage. Then she said with a rush. "It was your husband – my own father!"

Pearl gasped. "No! It couldn't have been! He was dead before you were pregnant!"

"No, Mum. I was in my very early stages when he died. He had been coming to my room nearly every night from the time I was ten!"

"Oh my God," Pearl had tears flowing down her cheeks. "I didn't know! I didn't know!"

Topaz nodded. "I know you didn't," she acknowledged. "He made me promise not to tell – told me it was my fault for coming on to him. Told me it was our secret."

Saffy hadn't moved. She looked devastated.

"The night the police came and told us he was dead, I was thrilled. At that time, I didn't know I was pregnant, but when I did, I decided to act the 'town bike' so you wouldn't know. I never actually had sex for years afterwards. I then felt guilty for not caring about Dad, for not caring for the men I brought home, for not caring for the baby that grew inside me. I put all that hatred into the child when she arrived."

Now Saffy was crying, too. Pearl moved around and they stood together, tears mingling as they just held one another.

Topaz continued.

"Later, when my singing career began to take off, I used the men that came along. Whatever they wanted they got – I already felt degraded anyway – a little more didn't hurt. Then I started to realise Saffy was my daughter and I loved her. I put all the perversions that I experienced down to achieving more in my career – saying to myself that it was for her. I hated myself then. The best thing I ever did, was walk out on Gus and '*The Blue Stocking*'. I never want to go back to that type of life again. I'm so sorry, Saffy, Mum."

Now Topaz began to sob again. It was a relief to let go of all the secrets that were in her heart.

"So sorry," she murmured again, lowering her head into her hands.

Pearl came around and put her arms around Topaz, and Saffy did as well.

The three of them stood like that for ages.

***

It was good to go and see Ruby. Jewel and Jade walked in, holding each others hands, and David was by their side.

"Hello, Ruby," Jade said. "You're looking a lot better today."

Ruby smiled.

"I haven't thanked you properly for helping Jade." Jewel added and David came around and kissed Ruby.

"No need," Ruby said. "I can't believe the Universe led me to this moment, and in the end I was able to find my daughter."

Jewel and David looked at each other over the top of Ruby's head.

"I don't think you should get too excited, Ruby." David mentioned. "Pearl is trying to find out exactly what happened in both of your pasts. She's being doing a lot of research, you know."

"Yes," agreed Jewel. "She told me the records were very scanty. It's been hard work for her. It also dredges up so many bad memories for her."

"It's OK," Ruby said as she held Jade's hand and sighed. "I just know. It's so wonderful! You'll see."

About fifteen minutes later, they could see Ruby was tiring. When Ruby's eyes kept flickering shut and eventually closed, they left quietly.

17.

The next day, Saffy approached her mother warily. The whole household had felt fragile since Topaz had told them the circumstances of her past. Pearl was still in shock, blaming herself for not knowing, not protecting her own daughter. Saffy didn't know what to feel.

Topaz seemed detached and miserable.

"Mum?" Topaz looked up. She had been vacantly staring at the kitchen bench.

"Mmm?"

"I need to talk to you."

Topaz nodded.

"Listen Mum, I don't blame you. It must have been Hell on Earth to keep all that to yourself. I know – that's how I felt when I thought I had killed Jade." She hesitated, then continued.

"While I was hiding, I met a lovely guy. I have to go and find him – tell him what has happened. I didn't even leave him a note – I just left. I really like him, and I should go and explain."

Topaz nodded again.

"OK." She didn't move.

Saffy stood and waited. She wasn't quite sure what she should do.

Topaz looked up. "Go!" she said. "I need you to be happy. Don't make the same mistakes I have."

"Oh, Mum." Saffy looked distressed. "Please don't feel that way. If I can forgive you, you must forgive yourself. Hate our father instead – he deserves it!"

Topaz sighed. "You're right, Sweetheart. Go and find this boy of yours and make amends. And if he wants to, I'd like to meet him and thank him for looking after you when you were at your lowest and unloved."

"Thanks, Mum." Saffy kissed her mother and gave her a hug. "I'm out of here! See you soon." And Saffy grinned and dashed out of the room. She whirled passed her grandmother who was sitting at her laptop staring at the screen.

"Yay! Oma! I'll see you soon."

***

When Saffy reached Rod's studio, she stood at the bottom of the stairs and hesitated.

What was she going to say? What if Rod wasn't home? What if he didn't want any more to do with her?

After all she had been through, this didn't seem so bad, so she gritted her teeth and climbed the stairs. She knocked on the door.

Rod answered before she had the time to change her mind. They stood looking at each other at the open door. Neither moved for what felt like forever. Then Rod said.

"What do you want?"

Saffy breathed again. "I've come to explain why I left so suddenly."

"You could have let me know since." Rod said

"Actually it wasn't as easy as that." Saffy admitted. "That's why I'm here now."

"OK." Rod swept his arm and bowed. "Come in, if you must!" He sounded a bit unhappy, mingled with a great deal of sarcasm. It was not very welcoming.

Saffy darted passed him and made for the beanbags in the corner. She sat down and curled her legs under her.

Rod sauntered over, and sat in the other beanbag, keeping his body stiff and his face disinterested.

Saffy began.

"When I went out, I fully expected to come home later, but I decided to go and see Ruby and find out if she would keep silent about my part in Jade's death. When I got there, I knocked on the door, but there was no answer, so I went around the back, found the door unlocked and went in. I found Ruby lying on the floor." Saffy stopped and took a breath, catching a sob before it could erupt.

Rod frowned.

He puckered his lips up and said, "So... You were hoping to do her a damage – this is exactly what you wanted, wasn't it?" He didn't seem a bit impressed.

Saffy nodded. "I know – but when I got there, all I could think of was helping her. She had no phone, and neither did I – I raced off and borrowed a phone at a shop and got the ambulance to her, then went back and stayed with her till they arrived."

Rod smiled stiffly. He spoke. "That's more like the Saffy I know – good for you!" He was still sarcastic, his eyes never leaving her face.

Saffy grinned thinly, the mirth not reaching her eyes. "Thanks!" She looked down at her hands. They were clasped so tightly you could see white around the knuckles. She tried to relax. "While I was waiting, Ruby told me that Jade was at home! After all my worry, I wasn't a criminal after all!"

Rod almost said, "*I told you so...*" but bit his tongue. He'd so often said that Saffy was probably imagining things worse than they actually were. He said nothing, however, merely nodded and encouraged her to continue.

Then Saffy told him about the awful revelations her mother had confessed earlier. His resistance slowly began to dissolve. It took Saffy some time to recount the horror of the news that her father was Topaz's father. She broke down several times and Rod had to wait until she could go on.

With every word that Saffy said to Rod, she was able to gradually face what she had learnt. It was hard though. She still found it difficult to reconcile the fact that her mother had lived with this knowledge for so long. That deep down Saffy had been right. Topaz had hated her, not her personally, but the reason she had come into the world. It made so much sense now.

The only thing that was still not computing inside her was that her mother told her that her feelings had changed – that Saffy *was* loved. She still marvelled that the accident and the subsequent results had changed them all. Would Topaz have ever told her the truth if Jade's accident hadn't happened?

Saffy stopped and looked at Rod. She didn't realise that tears were coursing down her cheeks, that she had been sitting and talking for nearly an hour. Rod was looking at her strangely.

"What?" She put her hand up to her face and looked at the wetness on her fingertips with surprise.

"Oh, Saffy." Rod said. "I'm so sorry!" Then he stood, came over to her and enveloped her in a hug so warm and comforting that Saffy cried even harder.

They stood together for what seemed hours, Saffy crying and Rod patting and soothing her, but it was probably only a few minutes in reality.

Eventually, as Saffy's sobs diminished into the occasional gulp, Rod held her away from him and tipped her chin up with his fingers so that she looked into his face. She felt the cool of air between them and felt bereft.

Her eyes looked into Rod's. They were red-rimmed and puffy and her face was streaked with lines of wet mascara, but Rod smiled.

"Come on," he said. "Let's have a nice comforting cup of hot chocolate. You'll feel better then."

Saffy sniffed. "I just want you to tell me you forgive me. I should have left a note!"

"You still worried about that?" Rod shook his head. "Stop being silly, of course I forgive you. I love you!"

There was a moment of complete silence while they both digested that bit of information. Rod couldn't believe he had said it out aloud, and Saffy couldn't believe she had heard it.

Then Saffy tried a weak giggle through the tears.

"Good thing I love you, too, then, isn't it?"

They never made it to the kitchen until about an hour later. Saffy was well and truly loved as they lay back onto the beanbags.

***

Pearl glared at the computer screen. She just couldn't find the information she so badly wanted.

At this point, her research had almost convinced her that her mother had died in the gas chambers of the Nazis. As far as she could make out, she had been taken from her mother's arms and given to the soldier, just before the group had been led into the gas chamber. She could almost feel her mother's anguish at being separated from her daughter. Little did her mother know in her unexpected last moments of trauma that the soldier's gallant act had saved the baby's life. Pearl had taken hours of research to backtrack along from her adoptive parents, to the soldier, to Auschwitz, to her mother.

However, as far as Ruby's background was concerned, it had been a much harder route. The adopting of concentration children had not been common knowledge, and the only other mention she could find was a very minor article by the commandant of the concentration camp of Buchenwald. It told of a young Jew girl who had a baby in the fields and that it had been the offspring of a German soldier. This fitted with the story that Ruby had told her. It seems that Ruby was the mother that had been working in the fields at the time of her daughter's birth.

Pearl had concluded that if all this was true, Pearl couldn't be Ruby's daughter. Where Ruby's child had gone was not documented. The difference in distance between Auschwitz and Buchenwald made it highly unlikely, however, that Ruby and Pearl were in anyway related. Especially in the light of the records showing her suspected mother had, in fact, died.

This left Pearl with a dilemma. Should she tell Ruby, or keep this information to herself? Or did she wait until they could convince Ruby to do a DNA test? It also made her heart ache for the woman that she thought had been her mother.

***

When Jade, Jewel and David left the hospital, they drove over to see Topaz, Saffy and Pearl.

The atmosphere inside the house was palpable. Pearl seemed cross, Topaz seems distant. Saffy was nowhere to be seen.

They all sat around in the lounge room, feeling uncomfortable. Finally Jade spoke.

"Where's Saffy? I came over to see her."

Pearl apologised. "I'm sorry," she said. "Things have gone a bit pear-shaped here today."

Jewel raised her eyebrows in a question.

Pearl continued. "Well, it's not up to me to tell you Topaz's side of the situation, but Saffy has gone out. Apparently there's a boy she met while she was 'hiding out'."

She said this last bit with the bite of sarcasm. "I also had a difficult morning on the computer. From everything I can find, it looks like I'm not Ruby's daughter, and I'm having a hard time wondering if I should say anything to her at the moment."

David noticed that Topaz still seemed distracted. He spoke to Pearl. "I've always found that honesty fixes a lot of things," and he reached over and grasped Jewel's hand.

"I really don't know. The evidence is still not definite, but it looks fairly conclusive."

Topaz still stared blankly.

David directed his next question to her.

"Topaz, I think I've got a friend who is looking for a singer with his group. Would you be interested?"

Topaz hardly made a sound. She shrugged. "Mmm."

David looked at Jewel. He spoke quietly. "Why don't you two girls go out and get a cuppa for everyone?"

Jewel understood. She immediately stood up.

"Come on, Tope," she said with false gaiety. "Let's go. You coming, too, Jade?"

She walked up to Topaz and held out her hand, and the three of then went into the kitchen. Topaz still seemed detached and distant.

Jewel crossed her arms and leant against the bench.

"Jade, can you get the mugs organised and put on the kettle, please?"

Jade looked at her mother and pulled a face at her in the direction of Topaz. Jewel gave an almost imperceptible nod, and Jade did as she was told.

Jewel looked at Topaz. "Right! What's going on?" she asked.

Topaz looked confused then seemed to pull herself out of the daze.

"Just leave it, Jewel."

"No!" retorted Jewel. "I'm not going to let you get away with that. Something's wrong, and you know what they say – a trouble shared is a trouble halved! Tell me!"

Jade silently slipped out of the room and went back into the lounge. She knew that Topaz and her mother needed the privacy. David smiled at her when she entered and patted the sofa next to him.

"Good girl. Come and sit here with me."

He turned to Pearl and continued the previous conversation. "What exactly did you find out? Let me have a look."

Pearl grabbed a pile of papers from the computer desk and came around and sat down heavily on the lounge chair opposite David and Jade.

"I can't be absolutely certain," she began, pausing as she rifled through her notes, " but it's pretty well a foregone conclusion that I am not Ruby's daughter."

"Oh? What sort of things did you find out that made you think that?" David asked.

Jade sat a little closer to David and rested her head on his shoulder as she listened. David was thrilled, but didn't say anything; he merely leaned a little more toward her to give support.

Pearl sighed.

"The first thing seems to suggest that we were in completely different camps, and, I think, my mother went into the gas chambers. It looks very much like I was at Auschwitz and Ruby was at Buchenwald."

"That's fairly conclusive then?" David used the inflection, making his statement more like a question.

"Yes," answered Pearl. "The problem is – I don't know how to tell Ruby. She was hoping so much, that she'll be devastated."

David nodded. "Yes, I understand. Don't tell her then. Why don't you leave it for another twenty-four hours, then make a decision. Perhaps you can try getting Ruby to be more up to date, and try to get her to have her DNA tested."

"That's a good idea," Pearl conceded. "I was actually thinking I'd wait until she was better and home from hospital. I'll have to try talking to her again about the ease of doing a DNA test. She wasn't willing to go the DNA route when I mentioned it before. I think she's decided I'm her daughter – and that is that in her mind!"

"Yes. I know what you mean. I think Ruby was so lonely, that she jumped to conclusions and doesn't really want to learn the truth. However, waiting until she is better and at home again is going to be better." David concurred with a nod.

***

In the kitchen Jewel was still trying to get Topaz to open up. Topaz wasn't looking at her friend; she was busying herself, putting on the kettle and arranging the mugs on the bench. It didn't matter that Jade had already done that. She just needed something to do. She shifted the mugs like a magician shifts the cups over a marble.

"Do you want tea or coffee?" Topaz asked, keeping her eyes on the bench as if there were specks of dirt on it that were annoying her.

"Don't change the subject," Jewel said. "Look, I'm here – I'll understand. Just tell me. Is it your mother? Are you sick of her being at your place? Is it Saffy? Has she gone again?"

Topaz lifted her head with a snap and glared at Jewel.

"No! Nothing like that!"

"Then it's something that's happened to you!" Jewel realised. "Did Gus tell you that you had your job back, and you don't want it? Did the doctor tell you that something's wrong? Did you have an argument with Saffy?" Topaz kept shaking her head. "Well, what?" Jewel was getting frustrated.

"Oh! Jewel! What am I going to do?" Topaz looked at her friend and tears welled up in her eyes.

Jewel went over to her straight away.

"Tell me – it can't be all that bad. I'll be here for you!"

"You don't understand!" wailed Topaz.

"No!" Jewel chuckled. "I can't if you don't tell me!"

With that, Topaz sat down on the kitchen stool and wept – stuttering out the story a little at a time.

Jewel listened patiently. She didn't interrupt, she didn't judge, she didn't even move. She just listened.

Eventually Topaz hiccoughed into silence.

Jewel came over to her and put her arms around her.

"You know. Tope, You are still you. Saffy is still Saffy, and Pearl is still Pearl. We are friends and that's that. The only bastard in this whole story is now dead and gone. Forgive yourself, Honey. It wasn't, and still isn't, your fault or Pearl's. You both had a hell of a plateful to put up with back then. It's going to be OK!"

Topaz looked up at her friend and tried to smile. Jewel handed her a tissue and smiled back. She knew that Topaz would now be able to start to heal, just as she had when David had listened to her.

The phone rang and shattered the moment.

Jewel called out to Pearl. "Pearl, can you get that, please?"

The jangle of the phone stopped and Pearl's voice could be heard.

"Yep!" …

"Of course." …

"Sorry, she can't come to the phone at the moment." …

"Yes, I'll let her know." …

"If you give me your number, I'll get her to ring you back."

…

"Thanks. Bye."

By the time the call had finished, Topaz had pulled herself together and wiped her eyes.

They put the kettle back on, and Jewel came out into the lounge to find out who wanted a drink. Pearl appeared to be busting to tell them something.

A few minutes later, cups in hand, they all congregated together.

Pearl, David, and Topaz all started to speak at the same time. Jewel held up her hands.

"Whoa!" She said. "One at a time! Please!"

They all laughed. David told Jewel the conclusions Pearl had come to, and that they were going to wait to tell Ruby, preferably when she came out of hospital. Topaz apologised for her mood when they had arrived, but said she felt a lot better now. Even Jade made the comment that it was great to have such a wonderful family around her. They all turned to Pearl.

"So!" Jewel queried. "Do you want to tell us about the phone call?"

"We..ell?" Pearl hesitated. She looked at Topaz and then at David. "First I want to thank David. Apparently that was a friend of his. Then," she turned to Topaz. "that was the lead guitarist of the band that plays at the local hotel. Their singer has just left, and wondered whether you would like to join the band. They have a contract to make an album and they don't want to break it. What do you think?"

Topaz swallowed nervously. "I'll talk it over with Saffy first. I won't even consider it if she doesn't want me to do it - but it's something I've always wanted to do."

While they were sitting drinking and discussing Topaz's offer, Saffy walked into the room. She seemed a little shy, and when everyone stopped talking and turned to her, she scuffed the carpet with her feet, bit her lip and said, with a minor flourish.

"This is Rod – he is my boyfriend." And Rod stepped out hesitantly from behind the wall where he had been hiding.

Topaz immediately stood and walked over to him.

"This is a pleasure. I'm so pleased to meet you. I believe you kept Saffy safe while she was at her lowest?"

Rod nodded, smiled and shrugged all at the same time. Saffy looked ridiculously proud and happy.

"Come and join us – do you want a drink? Anything to eat?" Topaz gushed.

Pearl looked at Rod with suspicion.

"What do you want from us?" she asked with a tilted eyebrow.

"Mum!" Topaz cautioned. "Don't."

Pearl just shook her head and went silent.

Saffy pulled Rod by the arm and sat him down next to Jewel, and then she gave Jade a hug and sat down next to her.

The conversation was a bit stilted, but slowly they went back to discussing the band offer.

"Please," Topaz stopped them all. "I want to ask Saffy's opinion."

Saffy actually grinned. It was the first time her mother had ever asked her to comment. It was like a light went off in her heart.

"Oh Mum," she said. "Whatever the offer is, it is something you must decide. I just want you to be happy!

"Good!" Topaz smiled. "As Saffy doesn't mind, I think I'll take up the offer. I'll put them on notice, though! They are on probation until I see if they are any good!"

Everyone laughed. That sounded much more like the Topaz they all knew.

**

Each day for the next week, one or another of them visited Ruby. They had set up a roster system.

Slowly but surely Ruby improved, until she was moved down to the general wards.

Just before Ruby was due to go home, Topaz visited her. Ruby appeared to be dozing when she arrived, so she quietly by the bed waiting for Ruby to awake.

Suddenly the machines began to beep and nurses came running.

Topaz had no idea what to do. She was asked to leave by one of the nurses, and as she backed away, the curtains were pulled around the bed so she had no clue what was happening.

No one came near her.

She felt rejected.

Worried.

Disregarded.

She tried to get someone to tell her what was happening, but the nurse said 'not now', and hurried in behind the curtain.

Topaz slowly left, walked down the corridor, found a waiting room and sat on one of the seats, staring into space. It seemed as if the whole world had fallen onto her shoulders. She hadn't realised how close she had come to the old lady.

It wasn't until some two hours had passed, that Topaz looked up and was surprised to see a senior nurse in front of her.

"Hi," the woman said quietly. "I know you were in with Mr Grebowski when everything became urgent and we had to ask you to leave."

When Topaz nodded, she continued. "I'm sorry. Unfortunately, Mrs Grebowski has had another heart attack."

Topaz gasped.

"Oh no! Is she OK?"

The nurse shook her head.

"I'm afraid that, although we have stabilised her, I don't think she has long. Perhaps you would like to get her family together and come and say your goodbyes."

Topaz gulped, tears blurring her vision. She didn't trust her voice.

The nurse looked at her with concern, but didn't move.

"OK." Topaz's answer was a whisper of shock. "I'll do it straight away."

Topaz got up and walked to the lifts. The nurse stood and watched her until she disappeared, then returned to her duties with a sigh. It was never easy to tell people that type of news, no matter how many times she had done it.

***

She stood trying to open the door of her car, still in a daze. She was finding it hard to process the bad news she had just received. She couldn't remember how she had got to the car park, either. When she wiped her eyes with her hand she realised she was trying to open someone else's car. She gave a weak giggle and looked around to see if anyone had seen her. Then she couldn't remember where she had parked her own car.

While her brain tried to find the necessary files to jog her memory, another thought popped into her mind.

"God, how could you be so stupid!" she castigated herself. She delved into her handbag and found her mobile. She called Pearl as well as Jewel, and told them the situation. She asked them to find everyone and come to the hospital – pronto. Then she slowly walked back to the entrance of the hospital and sat down to wait.

***

About an hour later, the whole group was standing in the foyer, all shocked by the news.

"But, Mum. I thought she was getting better." Jade was weeping. Jewel put her arms around her daughter.

"I know. We're all having trouble with the news. Try and dry your tears. When we go up and see Ruby, we don't want her to get upset."

Jade sniffed and nodded, taking a tissue that Pearl was offering.

Saffy was looking as if she was going to burst into tears any moment, as well. Rod held her hand tightly.

"I can't do this!" she said in a constricted voice. "I just know I won't be able to hold it together." And she turned and walked away.

Topaz was still dazed. Pearl took control.

"Come on, everyone. We all have to face this. This is life. There is no way I'm going to leave Ruby to face this alone. I'll even hold her hand if I can."

David came through the doors at that moment. He heard what Pearl said.

"Are you going to tell her what you have found out about her daughter?"

"No." Pearl said determinedly. "There is no way Ruby should hear the news that her daughter died. Not now. Not at this time. I'm not going to tell her anything."

Jewel was surprised.

"I didn't think you'd been able to trace that much," she said. "What happened?"

Pearl pursed her lips. "Sad, really. She became the ward of the commandant of the camp. Apparently she got the 'flu and wasn't hospitalised or medicated. She didn't even see her second birthday!"

There was silence. Nobody knew what to say. Pearl continued.

"I think, at this stage, we should let her think I'm her daughter. Will you all go along with it?"

They all nodded with understanding.

"After all, if she gets better, we can always tell her then – if not...."

Jewel took a deep breath.

"Well, I, for one agree – come on – let's not keep Ruby waiting!"

With that, they all, including Saffy, walked to the lift.

18.

At the funeral the weather was overcast and cold. They all gathered in front of the chapel.

"I think we've done the right thing," Jewel stated. "Being cremated would have been the last thing she would have wanted."

"I think it was marvellous that we found the documents at Ruby's place about Joseph." David remarked.

"Yeah," Pearl agreed. "To think she kept all the records of his funeral with the pictures on the altar thing she had."

"Well, now they're together." Topaz said. "At least we could do that for her – finding Joseph's grave and being able to get her buried next door to him was a stroke of wonderful luck."

"I'm still proud that you called her Mum," Saffy said to her grandmother. "It couldn't have been easy to do that, when you knew your real mother had been killed by the Nazis."

"Actually, it wasn't hard at all." Pearl commented. "It felt like she was my 'surrogate' mother, after learning what she had gone through."

Everyone nodded thoughtfully.

"Besides – it was worth it to see the smile that crossed her face when I said that." Pearl said. "I saw all the hurt disappear from her eyes, and her face became smooth and stress free."

"You know," Jade said with a sigh. "We didn't know her for long, but without her, I wonder if I would have been here?"

Topaz nodded.

"She was a wonderful lady and we were privileged to know her."

Then they linked arms and walked into the church.

About a week after I had finished writing this book, I stumbled (I randomly pick books at my local library) across the book called 'Magda's daughter' written by Catrin Collier.

I was stunned to learn that my memory of stories told to me in my youth (just after the war) had been correct.

Catrin had added a note at the back of her book telling of the Nazi Organization called 'Lebensborn'. Heinrich Himmler started this in 1935 to bolster the reducing population in Germany, and to recruit children to the Nazi ideal. Many children were 'kidnapped' from single woman who had children by German SS officers. If the Germans found 'Aryan' characteristics in any of the population they had conquered, they were taken as well. They were tested thoroughly and, if they didn't reach the ideals, were executed.

I have since done my own research into this, what I consider to be, criminal practise.

This book has been written under a pseudonym because this author normally writes for children. Obviously some of the content is not suitable for children. Her real name is Maureen Larter.

Facebook: facebook.com/ebooksbymaureenlarter
Twitter: @maureenlarter
Email: maureenlarter@gmail.com

ABOUT THE AUTHOR

 Maureen Larter was born in England in the late 1940's and came over to Australia when still a toddler. She is a teacher of piano and violin, and lives on the lower Mid North Coast of New South Wales, Australia. She lives on a small holding of 12 acres, and does her best to live self-sufficiently, while taking care of the soil and the environment. In her spare time she is learning to spin and weave. She has completed and received her certificates in 'Sustainable Agriculture' and 'Comprehensive Writing'. In the past, she has taught English, Social Studies, Music and Mathematics in High Schools within Australia. For a brief period she lived in China teaching English. While there she wrote a textbook for the students of the school.

She still teaches piano and violin.

On wet days, when she can't be out in her garden, and there are no students commandeering her time, she loves to sit and write. She writes children's stories and short stories, as well as occasional articles for magazines.

Other books written by Maureen:

Gardening Guides
- Summer
- Autumn
- Winter
- Spring

Short Stories
- Book 1 – At the Beach – (4 stories)
- Book 2 – Predicaments – (5 stories)

Books for young girls

Fairies from Aurora Village Series
1. Broken Wing.
2. Spiders ,Lizards and Flies
3. Cave of the Golden Bowerbird.

Kathy Edwards Adventure
In Search of the Elusive Panda

For Toddlers
Alphabet Animals of Australia Series
- Angus Ant and the Acrobats
- Betty Bee's Birthday Bash
- Ben Brolga's Band
- Candy Cow and the Caterpillar
- Cassie Crocodile Catches a Cold
- Dorothy Dog and the Dangerous Dragonfly
- Evie Emu's Encounter.
- Frank Frog Feels Foolish
- Giddy the Galah.
- Helen Heron and the Helicopter
- Iggy Ibis is Important.
- John Jabiru and the Jolly Jam tin
- Kathy Koala's Kerfuffle

This is an ongoing series. There are many more to come.

For all books, prices and more:- go to readeatdream.net
Also on Facebook, Twitter and Linkedin.
Email:- maureenlarter@gmail.com

www.ingramcontent.com/pod-product-compliance
Lightning Source LLC
Chambersburg PA
CBHW071109100726
47908CB00008B/2323